MW00713174

SCI PHI JOURNAL
Issue #5
May 2015

Art by Cat Leonard

Ebook Design by Jason Rennie

Edited by Jason Rennie, Lee Melling and Gene G. Glotzer

www.sciphijournal.com

editor@sciphijournal.com

Contents

From the Editor

Jason Rennie

A lot has happened since the last issue of the magazine. The podcast that spawned all of this, *The Sci Phi Show*, was nominated for a Hugo award and Lou Antonelli, who brought us the magnificent "On a Spiritual Plain" from Issue #2, also got nominated for a Hugo. There has also been a kerfuffle about the Sad Puppies campaign and all manner of ridiculous accusations going back and forth over the nominations this year. I have been blogging about this a bit over at SuperversiveSF.com. Thanks to anybody who nominated something Sci-Phi related for a Hugo. Your support is extremely encouraging.

Onto business, I have an exciting issue for you this time around. I always say that, but this one does have a couple of first-time features in it. I am very happy to say the first story in this issue, "The Keresztury TVirs" by Ivan Popov comes to us from Bulgaria via the Human Library Foundation and it is the first story I have run that has been translated from another language. I really hope you enjoy it. It is an honor to be able to bring his work to some small part of the English-speaking world. You can find out more about the Human Library Project at choveshkata.net. Also in this issue Josh Young, who gave us "Domo", the opening story from Issue #1, is back with "God Eaters", which is sure to entertain. We also have stories from Gregory L. Norris on the strange possibilities of cloning and from Scott Chaddon about what it might be like to be a god.

In our articles section, Patrick Baker is back with an article on civic militarism in Heinlein's "Starship Troopers", an idea I have always found very interesting, and Jeffrey A. Corkern is back again with the second of his essays on the search for the soul. We also have a great article on the Ring of Gyges and cloaking in Star Trek, by Victor Grech from Malta. You will also notice an ad for a Star Trek conference Dr Grech and his colleagues are hosting next year. Roy Gray fires the imagination with an article that asks why we are here and Anthony Marchetta is back with an article on the philosophy of *Serenity*, of *Firefly* fame.

I am also proud to publish L. Jagi Lamplighter's, "HMS Mangled Treasure" which was the inspiration for the cover art on this issue. It is a little bit of a change to our regular stories, as it has a bit more of a fantasy flavor to it.*HMS Mangled Treasure* is also the first explicitly Superversive story we have featured in Sci Phi, but you can look forward to more of those.

Ben Zwycky continues in very fine form with the next installment of "Beyond the Mist", which sees our character continuing his adventures and, based on empirical research Ben has done, this story doesn't just fire the imagination and adults, but is also excellent for stimulating the desire to read for children, at least if Ben's kids are anything to go by.

Finally Cat has outdone herself again producing a beautiful collection of art pieces to illustrate each of the stories in this issue. You will also notice Victor Grech's article has cover art as well, which he contributed himself.

So please enjoy this issue of *Sci Phi Journal*, and I hope it brings you as much pleasure reading it as it brings me to produce it.

Jason Rennie

Editor in Chief

Stories

THE
KERESZTURY
TVIRS

By Ivan Popov

Translated by Vladimir Poleganov,
Ivan Popov and Kalin M. Nenov

Andrew Keresztury. *World TVir History*. 4th edition

Springer-Verlag, Berlin-Istanbul-Islamabad-Singapore

#

The title of this book is slightly misleading. Or rather, the word "history" is misleading, bringing expectations of abstract moralizing and technical ignorance. However, the author—the TVirologist Andrew Keresztury—is an outright "techie"—one of the greatest experts in the field. That's why his book is in fact a thorough technical overview, disguised as a history out of decorum.

The disguise succeeded in confusing even the publishers, as the first edition was included in the Critique of Postmodernism series, and the blurb compared the book to Douglas Rushkoff's *Media Virus!* As a matter of fact, *World TVir History* saw the light of day only due to its publishers' confusion. TVirs are a rather delicate subject, and various secret services have made various aspects of their technical details top secret over time. Had it been classified as technical literature, the competent authorities would have stopped Keresztury's work long before it reached the bookstores. In this particular situation, however, the first edition of *TVir History* remained on the bookshelves for twenty-three days' before it was brought to the attention of the intelligence services and its entire print run was seized. The authorities went as far as tracing customers who bought copies from online bookstores and forcing them to return their purchases. In fact, this part of the book's history is no less intriguing and edifying than the story of the TViruses it tells. Nevertheless, let us focus on the contents of the work itself.

Keresztury begins his presentation directly with the question "Who is to blame?" and gives a fitting answer: everyone, or—tantamount to this—no one. There are, as the virologist calls them, certain objective causes: the obsession with digitization and protocol standardization, the developers' penchant for creating systems with a great number of extraordinarily powerful undocumented functions. To top it all, we have had incredibly "lousy" operating systems since Microsoft, overblown beyond all measure, which when released in firmware, require chips with an immense capacity. Moreover, any smart programmer can insert almost anything into the "small" amount of unused memory on the chips.

And this "anything", according to Kerezstury, has evolved greatly over time.

Historical sources cite the Ukrainian city of Odessa as the motherland of TVirs; the names of the first TVirmakers are well known: the hardware developers Leonid Kunitz and Miron Craciunescu (the latter is Moldavian). Kunitz and Craciunescu discovered by accident undocumented functions in digital TV sets, which allowed commands to be sent to the set via the cable along with the TV signal. More specifically, they were commands for upgrading—as well as tampering with—the firmware OS behind the back of the TV set's owner. Besides, it turned out that these functions had been an implicit standard, adopted by all manufacturers. So Kunitz and Craciunescu invented the mixer: a device placed on the cable before the TV set, convolving the appropriate commands into the signal (initially, this used to be a computer program, not a separate hardware device). The first virus they wrote was quite simple and mischievous: its functions included shaking and inverting the screen image, creating "snow"; it assigned these functions to certain button combinations from the remote control.

After spending considerable time experimenting with their own TV sets, the budding TVirmakers plugged a remote control mixer into the TV cable running along a block of flats and started terrorizing all the viewers in the neighborhood by inverting the picture during key scenes of the popular soap operas of the time. The viewers, naturally, showered the local cable operator with complaints. It did not take the technicians long to find the mixer, but instead of unplugging it, they played a Byzantine trick: they removed the battery and hid nearby, waiting for the TVirmakers to show up and fix the device, and then caught them with the help of some private security men. The unwitting Ukrainian court passed a surprisingly light sentence on Kunitz and Craciunescu: 10 days in custody for hooliganism using technical devices. However, the news about those "technical devices" spread like wildfire. The cable operators in Odessa started a full-blown war: they all installed mixers on their competitors' cables and inverted the picture using the Kunitz virus. They soon concluded a truce, but someone— perhaps even Kunitz or Craciunescu—released the virus code on the Internet, making it accessible to every hacker in both Eastern and Western Europe.

The second generation of TVirs brought along more complicated "user" functions, mainly to do with sound manipulation. At first, they were restricted to changes in the voice timbre and other similar effects; from a technical point of view, this was no easy feat, because the sound was digitally encoded and the manipulation algorithms were rather compact. The center of this new generation of TV infection was thought to be Romania. There is a story of one Traian Radulescu who caused his aunt to have a heart attack by making the delicate and beautiful actress in a movie declare her love in a hoarse drunkard's bass. Later, though, these effects became extremely popular, and cable operators themselves started installing them on TV sets at their clients' request. It turned out that people liked it: pressing buttons on their remotes and changing the actors' voices, the timbre of musical instruments and so on—replacing them with the weirdest substitutes.

Shortly afterwards came the first TViruses capable of inserting new lines into film dialogue. On the eve of the regional elections, a group calling itself the Maznev/Razmaznev TVir Crew unleashed a virus which, during the pauses, inserted various insults with a random timbre, aimed at one of the candidates: "Nevertheless, Artuchki is a swine!", "But we must keep in mind that Artuchki is a swine!", "The fact that Artuchki is a swine is indisputable," and so on. The name of that group featured the abbreviation "TVir" for the first time. (Keresztury makes no mention of the denigrated candidate's reaction.)

Over the next few years this type of virus evolved considerably and became a favorite weapon of radical political organizations across America and Europe. They were widely used by antiglobalists and neofascists, to mention but two examples. Besides the now conventional medium of remote control mixers plugged into cable networks, propaganda TVirs also spread via infected pirated DVDs. (The undocumented commands can infect a TV not only through the cable input but also through a random digital video recording.) These PropaTVirs caused the police serious trouble, and draconian measures were introduced, decreeing sanctions not only for the propagators but also for those who willingly installed broadcast-changing code in their TV sets. During one of its campaigns, Interpol arrested the members of the Maznev/Razmaznev group, but several weeks later the convicts managed to escape custody under mysterious circumstances and vanished into thin air. It was a good fifteen years later that a member of the group was discovered, accidentally shot during a police operation against the "white plastic" mafia in Germany.

Among the so-called active-sound TVirs, Keresztury includes certain minimalist, obscure ersatz versions, which do not have the line insert and voice change functions. For example, if the virus identifies the president's name in the signal, it emits noise in the channel and briefly deteriorates the picture quality. This behavior of the signal makes viewers angry, and their anger gradually projects onto the person mentioned—analogous to Pavlov's dog conditioning. It is interesting to note that these simpler active-sound versions appear later than their more complex predecessors. They have been used not so much by the radical fractions, but by election offices that would release the virus against their own candidate and subsequently charge their opponents with unlawful subliminal attacks.

Image-manipulating viruses appeared a good ten years after the sound-manipulating ones. According to Keresztury, this was due to the more complex and extensive program code required for image analysis. Once the TVOSs evolved sufficiently and the TV processors became fast enough, such viruses cropped up in the wild. As always, sheer hooliganism led the way—with "the mustache painter" (which, along with the entire algorithm for facial recognition, fits in a tight 36 kilobytes!). Later, the "sentence eraser" appeared, designed as a weapon against advertising. Next came Bayraktar[1] : a

---

[1]*bayraktar*—standard-bearer (Turkish). —translators' note

tiny figure, waving a red flag with a crossed hammer and crescent, which would jump out in a corner of the screen at those very instants when the video stream was at its dynamic peak. (Thereby mercilessly distracting the viewer's attention.) Bayraktar spawned a whole new brood of animated pests that switched on to torment the viewer on all kinds of occasions. Usually they formed part of an advertising campaign or counter-campaign.

The antiviral efforts of TV operators included the automatic distribution of anti-TVirs in their networks, which scanned the memory of the sets and wiped out the parasites. Programs for TV memory disinfection were also made available on the Internet. The TVirmakers responded with stealth TVirs, capable of completely disguising themselves. Furthermore, at a certain point TViruses became a fad: for example, teenagers who wanted to get back at their parents would infect the family TV sets, using special outer devices bought from the black market. The same market saw the advent of pre-TV boxes, which provided signal preprocessing along with the functionality of all viruses: sound manipulation, picture inversion, bouncing Bayraktar-type pest images, and even elements of AI, inserting moronic lines into movie dialogues and anchors' announcements.

According to Keresztury, the most outrageous aspect of the whole story is that the TV set manufacturers never eliminated the commands and functions which made TVirs possible. They neither agreed to restrict the standard, nor provided virologists with any explanation for the necessity of having such powerful and dangerous options in an ordinary household appliance. Consequently, the author makes the assumption that the manufacturers had been planning to use the millions of TV processors for their own purposes—to employ parallel computations and then harvest the results, for example. (At the time, there was an extremely popular rumor that any extra computational power of household devices was being used in such a manner.) It was only when the TVir epidemics broke out and spread that two or three TV models were introduced whose hardware disabled any TVOS upgrades. However, firstly, these models were not very popular, and secondly, the hardware deactivation could be reversed by soldering a single pin onto the circuit board.

The above does not contain any new or classified information: this has all been publicly available for a long time, and the author only deserves credit for gathering and systematizing it. Later in his book, however, Keresztury focuses on an entirely different type of TVir which had only been rumored to exist, without any substantiating facts or official statements. We refer to Tviruses that contain subliminal messages as a "user" function.

Subliminal suggestion techniques had been known since the previous century: a sound or a voice whose volume (or frequency) is just below the threshold of perception can still be perceived, although subconsciously. The same applies to images hidden in the video stream: by either using a 25th frame or dispersing the individual pixels over multiple frames. These techniques have long been developed by special services as a promising tool for "conviction pushing"—propaganda or advertising. But there is nothing, absolutely nothing, preventing their release as TVirs.

In fact, Keresztury provides no evidence that such TVirs have actually been created and propagated. He only outlines the basic scheme and denies the rumors that subliminal viruses had been employed by the once notorious dictator Julio Cesar Milletbashian. As some of you doubtlessly still remember, Milletbashian was overthrown after an international intervention, provoked by reports that he was secretly designing a new generation of psychomanipulating technologies in order to zombify his subjects.

Afterwards, however, no one could say what these technologies were, or whether they had existed at all. Keresztury, who at the time used to work for one of the departments responsible for Milletbashian's ousting, notes that in the country in question, due to the extremely low standard of living, digital TV sets were relatively rare, which means that the subliminal viruses would have only zombified the wealthy minority. Keresztury's department only discovered a few modified versions of standard TVirs of the Bayraktar and "Artuchki is a swine!" variety; furthermore, they had been used for campaigning against rather than for Milletbashian.

It has been commonly believed that the discussion of Milletbashian's viruses—or, to be more precise, of their nonexistence—led to the book's incrimination and its author's arrest, on a charge of disclosing top secret information. Indeed, almost all the information concerning Milletbashian used to be classified until recently. However, according to most experts, the real reason, the real bomb, is hidden in the penultimate chapter of the book where Keresztury describes hemisphere-switching videomodifiers (HSVM).

What is the general principle? It is a well-known fact that the brain has two hemispheres, each one inhibiting the other, so that at any moment one is dominant and the other is repressed. The left hemisphere is responsible for logic and speech, and the right for image perception. When a person is watching TV, especially if the picture is bright and dynamic, the right, irrational hemisphere is more excited and dominating, even in viewers whose left hemisphere is stronger. But Keresztury insists that if tiny, barely visible special changes (videomodifiers) are inserted into the TV picture, they would repress the right hemisphere and excite the left, which is the rational one. What is more, he sets out the exact technology for generating videomodifiers, along with all required formulae and algorithms.

The modifiers are visually perceived as weak disturbances in the picture just above the threshold of perception. Their subliminal component manages to subtly attract the viewer's attention. Thus some visual areas in the right hemisphere are repressed, and otherwise easy image processing is hindered—as if a filter or a silencer were installed in the brain. The disturbances are generated according to a complex geometrodynamic scheme. Keresztury says that he discovered the scheme in the files from the celebrated Asanovic trial, documented as a report on mental disorders caused by an unknown illegal video technology. The report had been prepared by an intelligence agent called Michael Singh. Later on, Keresztury discovered that a similar method had been developed by a pair of Ukrainian humanitarian technologists, surnamed Datsyuk and Yakimets, who were investigated in connection with the regime of dictator Milletbashian.

Keresztury concludes the section with the announcement that "quite recently"—that is, shortly before the book's first release in 2021—several TVir strains were discovered, employing videomodifiers using the Datsyuk and Yakimets method.

It was never explained, however, which strains these were. No one else has ever detected them. The print-run of the book was seized, the author arrested... but this was not the end of the story. A few months later, Keresztury was kidnapped by an armed group from the prison truck that was taking him to court. About two years later, a journalist came across Keresztury in the town of Berettyóújfalu at the Hungary-Romania border and even managed to interview him, but the mysterious TVirologist disappeared again.

Unlike his book, which literally days after the incrimination appeared as a file on various hardware sites on the Internet. The intelligence services acted swiftly against the online copies and even convicted three sysadmins who had been hosting the file on their networks. However, they found out much later that all their actions had been in vain. The book had become permanently available on websites in Bulgaria; but in order to remain undetected by search engines (and, in turn, the intelligence services), some of the letters in the file had been replaced by identical letters from the Cyrillic alphabet.

All of this was revealed after the end of the First World Humanitarian War, when the previously competent authorities were disbanded and the TV networks, or at least what remained of them, were transferred to the control of the World Great Jihad Organization. Given current television standards, the possibilities of virus infection have effectively been ruled out, and the balance of information intended for the left and right hemispheres is closely regulated according to the decrees of our leader and teacher, Ayatollah Mukadassi as-Sadr. Therefore nowadays Keresztury's work is of purely historical value—which has made its triple reprinting possible, thanks to the enormous amount of reader interest. Let us all hope that its value will always remain purely historical. Allah karim!

#

Jallal Masudi

Thracian Kurdistan Book Review (Eski Zagara Hisar)[2] , vol. 152/2059

Translated from the Kurdish by Ovanes Papazian[3]

---

[2]The old Turkish name for the Bulgarian town of Stara Zagora. —translators' note

[3]Armenian version of the author's name (Ivan Popov). —translators' note

14

Food for Thought

What is the future of television—an ordinary or Internet-based one? How can it be used to influence our opinions and daily choices? How can we turn the tables on those who try to manipulate us? Can anything be done to prevent an outcome along these lines?

About the Author

Ivan Popov is a translator and former physics researcher who lives and writes in Sofia, Bulgaria. His short stories and futurological essays have been published in various Bulgarian anthologies. His first novel, Хакери на човешките души (_Hackers of Human Souls_), was published in 2004.

choveshkata.net
The Human Library Foundation

is a non-profit association of
Bulgarian writers, translators and
avid readers whose mission is to
promote human-evolving fiction
both in Bulgaria and around the world.
We act in three major directions:

*1. Selecting, publishing, promoting and distributing the eponymous
Human Library series in Bulgaria, whose titles are chosen not by their
genre or themes but by their focus on what makes us human, and what
can bring us to the next stage along our road. The series includes works
by Peter S. Beagle, Theodore Sturgeon and various Bulgarian writers.*

*2. Publishing, promoting and distributing ФантAstika Almanac
in Bulgaria: a yearly anthology devoted to fiction, critique and facts related
to all forms of the fantastic, with an emphasis on speculative fiction.*

3. Selecting, translating & promoting Bulgarian literature around the world.

Along with our sister organization, **Terra Fantasia Association of
SF Writers and Artists,** we are actively seeking European partners for
joint projects under the EU Culture Programme 2014-2020 and other
international collaborations. If you are interested—e.g. in having your
country's speculative fiction translated and published in Bulgaria,
or participating in the European Fantastival (a pan-European SF festival)
please find us at **poslednorog@gmail.com.**

Find out more on: http://choveshkata.net/blog/?page_id=36#English

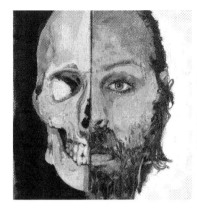

GOD EATERS

By Joshua M. Young

"That one, there," Peiromai said, voice hushed, almost reverent, "there's a god aboard it." He pointed out the flight deck window at a medium sized c-ship, too small for a god. Peiromai spoke of impossibilities.

"The Kadmon," I said. The Kadmon was only a demigod, but ancient and powerful and steeped in legend. Birthed by the Pinakes, the Library Goddess; older than his creator, her lover and her child —the gods were incestuous, both sexually and chronologically— and I'd eat him with the same relish that I'd consume his progenitor-lover.

But my own lover shook his head. "No, a god. Something older than the Kadmon, wiser than the Pinakes."

"Nothing is older than the Kadmon."

"Nothing human," Peiromai said. "It's an alien god we'll eat tonight."

#

The world where we had found the Kadmon had been chosen carefully. It was prosperous enough to have traffic, but not so advanced or prosperous as to control that traffic. When we seeded the orbit with passive dust, no one took notice; when the dust

17

became active in the vicinity of the Kadmon and detonated, no one responded. Those who were there chose to look the other way. A great many c-traders had developed keen self-preservation instincts in the gigaseconds spent trading.

The Kadmon's ship was a tough thing, not so fragile as to be crippled by something like dust. It could certainly be staggered, however; and when Peiromai and I boarded, it was unable to defend itself.

The Kadmon was another story altogether. One arm was charred and shattered, his face bloody, cooling fins erupting from his back as his bones struggled to repair the injuries. My mouth watered at the ozone-smell of smart matter.

Even injured, even missing an arm, the Kadmon was a force of nature. He fell on us moments after boarding his ship, lashing out at Peiromai with a meter-long smart matter blade. The stroke rent Peiromai's boarding armor; the backstroke nearly took off both our heads. Peiromai fell backwards; I dove to the side and gained a shallow gash on the throat, cauterized with waste heat from the blade.

Peiromai lashed out with a monofilament whip, but the Kadmon dove forward, losing the tips of his cooling fins instead of his own head. A flawless roll made suddenly awkward by the fins brought him up within Peiromai's arms, and the blade went through the underside of my mate's chin and out through his skull. A blur of movement, and Peiromai's head fell apart like a melon.

Hunger and rage threw me at the Kadmon, teeth bared, the array of god-killing weapons that would preserve the precious smart matter, forgotten.

The Kadmon was merciful. The dregs of rationality inside my skull expected a blade through the eye; instead, it went through my heart. Debilitating, crippling, but the all-important brain remained intact.

The pain, though, was impressive.

#

My time-sense was gone, the forever ticking digits behind my eyelids absent for the first time in memory. My bone-self had gone quiet, no longer whispering to me, offering hints about the universe. I had become the Kadmon's prisoner, arms stretched out to either side, hands embedded all the way to the wrist inside the wall. He had at least allowed me to sit and enough flexibility to shift from one numb buttock to the other.

The Kadmon was hale and whole, no longer missing his arm; his expression was serene, but his hair was damp and shiny lumps of med gel were visible near his collar. He'd likely spent more than a little time immersed in a med vat. I wondered about my own wounds, but before I could ask, the Kadmon said, "Ushki. God-eaters. You know who I am?"

"An ape ascended to godhood. The pet of the bitch-goddess, the Pin—"

He crouched slowly, a thoughtful look on his face until the very moment he slammed my head into the wall. I grinned, trying desperately to ignore the pain, and said, "And dinner. I can smell your bone-self, ur-human. The scent of the smart matter in your marrow. I'll crack you open and feast on the god-tech inside you while your flesh rots."

Hatred and disgust mingled in his eyes. I knew what he was seeing. Utterly hairless, digits that were more talons than fingers, skin turned gunmetal by the saturation of smart matter. Baselines, and those who kept the baseline form, rarely viewed the ushki as human.

19

"I don't know what to do with you."

"I know what to do with you," I told him, and licked my lips.

For a long moment, I thought he might kill me. But the moment passed and the Kadmon shook his head and turned away. His back was smooth and utterly human. The cooling fins would've retreated back into his bones when the crisis and aftermath had resolved.

"You gods," I spat. "Pretending you're human. Even your bitch puts on a human shell. You may have been born on the Cradle, Kadmon, but you're less human than I am."

"And yet," the Kadmon said, "Were you in my position, you'd be cracking open my femur as we speak."

Not a lot of use arguing that one, I suppose.

#

After some time, the ship-lights went down, and I dozed fitfully. The weight of my body pulled uncomfortably on my shoulders and wrists, and sleep was hard in coming and harder in staying. When morning came, I opened my eyes to find the Kadmon crouching next to me.

"I'm going to let you loose," he said, "On the condition that you behave yourself."

"If I don't?"

The Kadmon's eyebrows inched up. "An interesting consequence of your particular mode of enhancement is that the smart matter in your body is cohesive, but only just. You might as well have an abacus installed in your bone-self, for all the computing power you leverage. But that's what you get with stolen smart matter, I guess. It doesn't really like talking to the other stuff inside you."

"And?"

"I spent the night hacking your bone-self. You try anything, and I'll break the cohesion of your smart matter. The nanomachines in your bones will begin attacking each other, and you will likely die a very painful death."

The wall pushed my hands up and out, and I wondered if it'd been waiting for a cue from the Kadmon or if it was sentient enough to have a sense of dramatic timing. I rubbed my wrists, tried to flex my shoulders. "What's to become of me, if I behave?"

"I'm burning for a fairly low-tech world right now. A dozen megaseconds or so, ship-time. You'll be left there with your bone-self in a deadened state. Your ship I'll sell somewhere further down the line. Until we get to your destination, you'll be a guest."

"You could kill me, save yourself the trip."

"I could," the Kadmon agreed.

#

The Kadmon locked himself away for a short time each ship-day. The same room each and every day; located in the living area of the ship and locked at all times.

It was perhaps a day and a half before hunger and rage overcame me; I prowled the corridors and, finally, when the Kadmon emerged from his sequestration, I attacked. By all rights, I should've died then and there, but he had placed far too much faith in either my self-preservation or my integrity. I took him by surprise and drove his skull against the bulkhead. Wood paneling shattered and the Kadmon slumped to the ground. For a moment, I considered how best to butcher him, whether to leave him living to witness me eating his bones. Peiromai's blood called for...

The door hung ajar. Inside, I caught a glimpse of red carpeting and the same dark wood that was paneling the walls. The room inside was sparsely decorated, a handful of unfamiliar symbols

21

carved into the wood. A pair of intersecting wooden beams hung above a cabinet, once gilded and ornately carved; now scorched and vacuum ablated, sat on a dais opposite the door, a candle sheathed in red glass burned next to it. I felt in some subtle way, that I was intruding on something.

"It's an alien god," Peiromai had said. Words forgotten in a hunt gone terribly wrong.

I had invaded a ship, intending to attack and mutilate its owner, all without qualm; now, I felt wrong.

An alien god. Something unknowable, inhuman. The Kadmon had enshrined it; evidently worshiped it. Some sort of subtle brainwashing, an energy field flooding the room. I took a step towards the shrine, felt my knees buckle. I'd just driven the head of a god through a wall, but I felt unaccountably weak, blood streaming from my nose and eyes and ears, through my pores, grayish red with hemorrhaged smart matter...

The Kadmon's alien god was a conqueror, hostile. My legs finally gave, and I fell onto the dais, an outstretched, bloody arm knocking the god from its perch. Pale wafers cascaded out and onto the carpet.

It was only as I fell that I realized the Kadmon was standing in the doorway. For the first time, I felt fear when I met his eyes.

He hauled me off the ground by the collar. I felt fabric stretch and tear, but it held. Only just; in its deadened state, my bone-self couldn't coordinate reinforcement.

"You have no idea, god-eater, how much I want to kill you."

"Then do it," I snapped. "Decaseconds ago you told my bone-self to kill me. Then you stopped it. Why? Just finish it. Save yourself the trip."

He opened his fist; the deck hit me hard and I gasped.

"Clean up your blood."

#

The Kadmon and I dined later in the ship-day on fresh foods procured from the world of our ill-fated ambush. He ate with quiet grace; I ate awkwardly, picking at some nameless fruit and thinking of smart matter, warm, slick with fresh blood. My mouth watered, but my stomach turned as I thought of my own smart matter-laden blood oozing from my skin.

"I hate you," the Kadmon said, "I hate your people for what they once did to me. For what they did to others. But that was a long time ago and a long way away. Your people aren't what they once were."

I looked up, surprised. His words were quiet and conversational, as if we'd been pleasantly talking the whole meal.

"You're worse. Before, you were a bunch of trust-fund-kids playing at archeology. Now you're pirates, cannibals."

"Why don't you kill me?" I felt my eyes moisten, and I cursed the deadened state of my bone-self. I was stressed and had no way of controlling it.

"I would've earlier, if you'd been anywhere else. But that place has been dedicated to the Living God. It's not a place for death."

"And now you're not killing me, why?"

"Because I am a human being, not an animal. To kill you now would be to succumb to my hatred, to be a machine of meat souped up with smart matter. The Living God made me better than that. Better than instinct and emotion."

"Why do you call the Pinakes that?" I asked.

"The Pinakes isn't a god," he said. "She didn't make me; she healed me when I was mostly dead. She is wise and beautiful and I love her, but, ultimately, she is still a human soul inside a matroishka brain."

The Kadmon told me a ridiculous Cradle legend about the origin of the universe and a god who didn't start human and ended up being made of bread and wine after he became human, in order to die. The Kadmon was the last of this god's worshippers, and the god salvaged from a broken space station, teraseconds old.

At the end of it all, I mocked him, clapping my hands and shouting, "You, Kadmon... you're nothing more than a god-eater!"

I expected him to lash out. Instead, he laughed and cleared his plate from the table.

I sat alone in the mess for a while, a bowl of unfamiliar fruit on the table in front of me. I was stung by my failure to truly needle the Kadmon, irritated by the fruit whose names I didn't know. Did I even know the name of the world? Maybe my bone-self could've told me, but the fact of the matter was that it had been Peiromai who had made the choices since we mated; my parents before that. I was a creature of hunger and instinct, thoughtless reflex.

A machine of meat.

Less human that the Kadmon. Less human than one of the hated gods.

#

The Living God was not very lively, all things considered. The Kadmon left the door to his altar unlocked now, and I regularly watched him kneel and meditate with his hands clasped in front of his chest, without any apparent concern for his safety. After a kilosecond or so of this, he would consume his deity's body and drink his blood. The origins of the ushki hunger are opaque to me,

24

but I knew that one does not worship a god by eating them.

The Kadmon, I realized one morning, had made a habit of misplaced trust. In his god of bread and wine, in me, in his ability to dominate software and smart matter. Strange symbols barraged me when I first opened my eyes, and it took a bewildered decasecond to understand that this was my time-sense, once again active and desperately begging for input from a standardized pulsar in order to function accurately. It is perhaps true that the harvested smart matter in the ushki body is, at best, tenuously connected, but every child is born with a bead of indigenous smart matter formed in the womb. It is this organ that enslaves the harvested material. It is this organ that had been chipping away, silently, at the Kadmon's unattended slaveware.

I held my hand in front of my face and flexed my fingers. An array of tools emerged from my skin with each flex: blades and monofilament whips and half a dozen data interfaces.

No primitives for me. No life of starvation. I let the image of the Kadmon, butchered and stripped of smart matter, blood seeping into the carpet of his sanctuary, play through my head. The ozone-smell of my own smart matter whipped my appetite into a frenzy and I fought to keep it down, to bring it back into check. It would be an animal's reaction to stalk the Kadmon now, stupid and instinctual. Keep it low-key, keep it routine, wait, wait for the chance to strike, be human...

#

I considered the Living God's altar, and then dismissed it. For all his apparent vulnerability, the Kadmon had been surprised there once already. I could not imagine that he would not have prepared some sort of defense during his meditations. But then, twice I'd tried to kill the Kadmon; why should any place be any less defensible. The Kadmon's confidence was a weakness, but I was certain that he would not have a baseless confidence. I liked the idea of the altar; there was something poetically just about destroying someone as foolish as the Kadmon at the foot of a foolish alien god who became human just to die.

Several ship-days passed, three hundred kiloseconds or more, my time-sense forever begging for the pulsar synchronization, my bone-self whispering more and more in my ear, hunger growing with every second.

Be human, be rational. Plan.

The Kadmon meditated, and I watched. The ship drew ever closer to the world in which the Kadmon planned to imprison me.

More than machine. More than hunger. Act only when the time is right.

"If you are going do something," the Kadmon finally said, from his knees, his back to me, his hands clasped before his god, "now is as good a time as any."

A whiff of ozone and a blade—I hadn't realized existed—dissolved back into smart matter. "You said this isn't a place for killing."

"It's a fine place for killing," he said, a trace of humor in his voice, and I remembered the Living God's death, nailed to his own holy symbol, "it's just not a good place for me to kill you."

"You killed my mate."

"Did you love him?"

"What kind of question is that?!"

"A straightforward one."

"Does it matter? He was my mate!"

"The more like gods you folks become, the less like humans you are. You're viruses, ushki god-eater, attacking the individuals who link and preserve civilization in the galaxy. There'd be no star travel without individuals like the Pinakes, and you'd devour her in a heartbeat, if you could."

I leapt at the Kadmon, a long stabbing blade of smart matter emerging from my open palm. It went through his torso, just slightly off-center, and he fell forward. I dissolved the blade, kicked the Kadmon on to his back, began pummeling him.

"How could you?" I demanded, punctuating each word with a blow. My bone-self did nothing to regulate the flow of emotion; hate and rage and hunger overpowering my internal software. "You, here, lording over mortals, holier than thou, hoarding your technology for yourselves! You killed a human being and didn't even flinch!"

And then my mouth was full of the Kadmon's flesh and smart matter and there was a moment of sudden stillness, the Kadmon not struggling, I not devouring.

"Tell me this is human," he said.

My stomach cramped; when I clutched at my side, he said, "Fight it. Prove that you're better than your hunger. Prove to me that you're human."

Human, rational, plan, don't succumb, don't give in, don't lash out. . . .

Lash out I did, a monofilament whip unspooling with a vicious slash of an arm, but it went wide, I didn't kill him, the Living God's holy symbol falling in two. Tears, hot with rage and frustration and mixed with the Kadmon's blood ran down my cheeks. After a moment, maybe a decasecond, the Kadmon pulled my head to his chest, stroking my scalp with awkward, jerky movements.

"It's okay," he whispered, "I'm proud. You're doing good, you're

27

just fine. . . ."

In that moment, I knew I had missed on purpose. I wrapped my arms around him and pressed my cheek against his battered flesh. "The hunger, Kadmon. It's always there. Always gnawing. How did we get to be like this? We were normal people once, weren't we?"

He pondered this for a moment, hesitating for a fraction of a second before he spoke. "I suspect that your ancestors found that scavenger archeology wasn't getting them where they wanted to be —"

"Where was that?"

"The legendary home of the gods," the Kadmon said, "The Cradle. Earth, from where all our ancestors hail."

"And you."

"It was a long time ago. I suppose that your ancestors assumed that a more aggressive archeological method would locate the Cradle faster. Harvest smart matter and index the data fragments in it. The rest of it... Maybe the fastest way to index that data was internally. Maybe," and here he glanced up at the altar, "they sought to participate in the nature of the gods and find the place that way."

"Kadmon..."

"Yes?"

"Kill me?"

I felt his muscles tense. "Please," I begged him. "I can't live like this, not as a . . . god-eater. A cannibal, always starving. Death is better than that world you'll leave me on."

"If," the Kadmon drew the word out, as though buying time to think, "If I could help you, rid you of those instincts—"

"You'd change my very nature?" My stomach cramped again, and

28

I fought down a wave of nausea and hunger, as though my body were rebelling against the thought. "Will you take my memories, too?"

"No. Those you keep; to wipe your thoughts would be death."

#

The medical bath was a horizontal tube of transparent material, empty and hinged open. I sat inside, naked, freezing, fighting the urge to cover myself in the Kadmon's presence. For his part, he was a gentleman, or else revolted by the ushki form. He sat on the edge, patiently explaining what would happen during my return to the baseline body of my ancestors. "The Pinakes herself printed my ship," he said, "and the sick bay knows what it's doing. The uniquely ushki organs and features of your body will be removed or altered to baseline. I imagine that your bone-self will fight hard against reprogramming, and that it'll take some time for everything to shake out properly. Maybe megaseconds. But in the end, I think you'll come out okay."

I nodded, shivered.

"Sorry it's so cold. I don't know why these things are always like that."

I shrugged.

"Ushki."

"Yes?"

"I've never asked your name."

I opened my mouth, but the thought of my old life tasted foul. "It doesn't matter. Name me, Kadmon. Give me a name for my new life."

The Kadmon laughed. "Anastasia, then," he said, as if he expected

29

me to know what it meant.

"It'll do. Flood the tube, Kadmon. Wash away what I was."

Food for Thought

What do you make of Joshua's tale of a human being in need of redemption? For those who don't know, the name Anastasia comes from the Greek word *anastasis* which means resurrection, literally "to stand up". What do you make of the two conceptions of man embodied in the story? The cannibal god-eater driven only by cunning and hunger, and the higher nobler conception of man capable of rising above this basic nature and drive? Which is the real nature of man? Can Anastasia overcome her former nature with the help of Kadmon?

About the Author

Joshua M. Young is a Master of Divinity student at Ashland Theological Seminary in Columbus, Ohio. He suffers from such a crippling addiction to researching unfamiliar concepts, words, and cooking show mystery ingredients that his wife has suggested he give up Google for Lent next year. He can be found at thebadgercontemplates.wordpress.com and is the author of the forthcoming novel, *Buddhas Dream of Enlightened Sheep*.

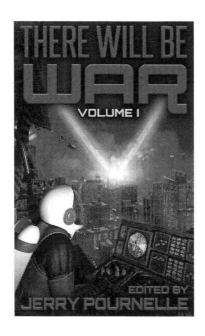 

The triumphant return of the bestselling 1980s anthology series of military fact and science fiction edited by SF living legend Dr. Jerry Pournelle.

Featuring classic short fiction from Orson Scott Card, Joel Rosenberg, Poul Anderson, Spider Robinson, Larry Niven and Jerry Pournelle, Philip K. Dick, and many others.

CASTALIA HOUSE

www.castaliahouse.com

GEORGE
THE
SECOND
by Gregory L. Norris

I heard my old neighbors the Henrys won the lottery. The news got delivered through a twisting and circuitous grapevine—an h-mail from a friend of a friend, which sent me on a net search to a short article with a buried headline. They don't like to make that stuff too public. Too many religious nut jobs out there, eager to form protest lines with placards or, worse, strap on a vest packed with explosives.

The Henrys beat the odds and scored. Better chances of being savaged by a live shark or flattened by a chunk of careening space debris, I read in my attempt to corroborate the truth. I suppose it would have been easier just to call. After nineteen years, I remembered their phone number. Couldn't tell you mine, but the Henrys' was branded into my grey matter.

They won the lottery. George Henry was an only child, which, I'm sure, meant they saved clippings from haircuts or banked blood and other genetic samples. I was the fourth of five; my parents stopped paying into the No Child Lost repository after my brother Cal, their third.

There was a new George Curtis Henry living at Number 17 Willow Lane. The first died nineteen years ago in a car wreck that claimed my best friend's life.

I hadn't been back to that town since the year of the accident, when Al Packer hit a patch of wet leaves left over from the winter on Barron Drive and slammed into a stand of maples growing at the inside edge of the sidewalk. Packer was speeding in excess of twenty miles over the posted limit on a twisting slope where ten was dangerous. The owner of the house where the car came to rest said he kept meaning to take out those trees, and the trees themselves may have been the culprits who shed the leaves that Packer's wheels slipped on. Maybe those maples were thirsty for human blood. Whether by design or accident, George wasn't wearing his seatbelt and got ejected through the windshield. Al Packer was charged with vehicular manslaughter, second-degree; speeding, and driving too fast for conditions. He pleaded guilty and was sentenced to three years' jail time—suspended. He lost his license for a year, and that was that.

I didn't like Al Packer and, to be honest, I didn't much like George that year for hanging around with him. I knew why George assumed the role of sidekick to Packer, who wore sleeveless muscle shirts and exuded a smell of motor oil. Packer was a gearhead and drove an old sports car that was slowly being restored over the course of our senior year. Childish on my part, I know, but we started spending less and less time together, and I resented George for it. The drift was inevitable, I'm sure, even if Al Packer had driven slower or taken a different route on a day that now seems impossibly distant, part of some other life.

We lived at Number 19. My parents sold the house and the

family scattered to different towns and states. I heard from half at Christmas, got h-cards on my birthday from the rest.

I'm not sure what I went back there looking for. The easy answer was curiosity. The brain trust that regulated the lottery maintained a tighter fist on the tech than practically any other, except nuclear and the new gray weaponry programs. I'm sure the Henrys put together an inspiring and emotionally-steeped package, likely endorsed with letters of recommendation from senators and celebrities alike. What was a reborn-person really like, in the flesh? Sure, we'd all seen the tawdrier exposés about human cloning on h-TV when it came to actors and rock stars, which helped pioneer the technology. But a real person? One who was an integral part of my history? A friend I loved? In some ways, George wasn't the only one who'd died in that car crash. None of us who attended his funeral were ever whole again.

Closure, more than anything, I suppose. I wanted to see George, my first and only best friend, again. Didn't matter that more than half a lifetime had passed since the last time he was alive, or that the world had changed so drastically since my years on Willow Lane. I gassed up the car on a full tank of high-test gellets and drove the distance, feeling the weight of years with the miles.

And then I found myself on Barron, motoring over asphalt I hadn't traveled in nearly two decades. The houses had changed. The road reached that place where it dipped down the hill. I drove, fell, spiraled. I didn't speed. The road was dry, free of wet leaves. Still, to part of me—the soul, perhaps—it felt like spilling over Niagara Falls, or reentry into the Earth's atmosphere. The bottom of the world dropped out, leaving me hanging over a black hole. I struggled for breaths that refused to come easily. A tenth of a mile over pavement that might as well have been an Astronomical Unit. Down the road. Time and space inverted. I suddenly felt younger and then, in the next second, much older.

I reached the trees that had claimed the first George Henry's young life. The house owner hadn't made good on his promise to remove them. The maples were far taller now, the kind of giants that haunt nightmares. I drove past them, eyes wide and unblinking, convinced they were about to reach out and make a grab at me, thirsty for my blood, too.

I made two more turns and entered the back end of my old neighborhood. My family was long gone from Willow Lane, and an odd sense of indifference replaced the eerie emotions unleashed on my cruise down Barron Drive. Two houses later, a sob hitched in my throat. To my right, the split-level ranch was as pristine-white as I remembered, the shutters a crisp black. Right as I passed and the sting of tears invaded my eyes, plunging the world beneath a flood only I could see, I caught a flash of motion from the periphery as a figure moved into the house. A boy dressed in blue jeans, new sneakers, and a checked shirt.

"Oh my God," I gasped. "George."

I continued past the Henrys' house, until the tears made it necessary to pull over. Farther up the road, I wept in a way I hadn't since the day of my best friend's funeral.

#

Turn around, I told myself. Park in the driveway—my sad, banged up relic of the past, running on hybrid gas pellets, beside the clean-burning vehicle I saw in that splinter of a second right before gazing upon George. Surely, the Henrys would be happy to see me, an old friend. But would my old/new friend? I wasn't sure, so I drove away after the shakes passed.

I took a room at a hotel one town over—nothing fancy—and ate a decent meal at a nearby restaurant. The sautéed vegetables had taste, and the salad's leafy components were green. There was that to be grateful for.

It stayed lighter longer now that it was spring. I thought about swimming in the hotel's pool or roasting in the sauna. But I hadn't driven all this way, spent a fortune on gellets, to sweat or soak. After splashing water on my face up in my hotel room, I headed out again in my car. This time, I parked in the Henrys' driveway right as it was getting dark and marched up the path of stone pavers leading to their front door. I rang the bell and willed my galloping pulse to calm. Breathing again stopped being easy or even involuntary. It never occurred to me what I would say if a younger version of my friend were to answer the door.

He didn't.

The outside light switched on, bathing me in a burnished yellow glow. An older woman drew the door open. I knew she was Sylvia Henry—short, pretty, a familiar face that had fast-forwarded through time.

"Yes?" she asked, eyes narrowed.

In the spotlight, I realized I was a stranger now, disconnected from Willow Lane by almost two decades. "Mrs. Henry," I said, and flashed a nervous smile. "Not sure if you remember me."

But she did, and spoke my name. She smiled, too, though I could tell the gesture came with hesitation. Mrs. Henry took a heavy swallow, her body language impossible to misread.

"I wanted," I said, "you know, I heard about—" The sentence went unfinished. "If this is a bad time, I can come back."

"You're here to see George," she said. I didn't know how to respond, so I didn't. Right when I decided to turn and leave, she welcomed me into the house.

37

I remembered Mr. Henry as having neat, dark hair. The man sitting in one of the two-patterned, overstuffed easy chairs across from the sofa sported a close-cropped head of silver.

"You have to understand, we need to be cautious," Mr. Henry said.

"Sure," I nodded, aware of the gesture, of the lone word I uttered. But my consciousness had jumped out of my body, and the exchange was made with a disconnected quality.

I hadn't been in this house in years, but it was, I swore, the same —a mirrored curio shelf over the sofa populated by figurines from Europe, bunches of silk flowers, the familiar grandfather clock whose ticks defied time more than tolled it, and large family photographs in frames. Only I wasn't sure if the school snapshot of George Henry belonged to the dead version or the new.

"We heard you got on TV," Mrs. Henry said. "How exciting."

"Me and everybody else out there," I said. "It was that stupid cook-off, Slice or Dice. I got diced in the third episode."

"How are your folks?"

I thought about shrugging. Instead, I lied. "They're doing great. Does he know?"

"About what happened?" This, from Mr. Henry. I nodded. "We've been upfront with George. The lottery urges you to let them know exactly where they've come from, like in traditional adoptions. Other kids can be cruel, you know. It could come up at school."

"Does he know about me?"

The Henrys exchanged a look that told me George didn't.

"George, he's . . ." Mrs. Henry started.

My smile crumbled. "It's okay. If I were such a good friend, I wouldn't have let him get in Al Packer's car to begin with. I would have stopped it before it happened."

"You couldn't have. And you were a good friend," she said.

I rose from their sofa. The room attempted to spin around me. A deep breath, and the effects of the time warp stopped. My muscles felt whole again. "It was great seeing you, but I should go."

I headed across the living room.

"No, wait," Mister Henry said. "George'll be home soon. He's studying with a friend."

A good friend, I figured. The best. After their loss and winning the lottery, I was sure the Henrys had kept their son on a very short leash. Curfews and routine consultations with the parents of any potential friend. A friend who didn't speed, who obeyed rules to the letter. I wanted to feel jealous, but the most I managed was relief. The Henrys—and especially their second George—deserved a level of certainty. Their family had suffered enough for one lifetime, let alone two.

I started to respond—better for me to go before George returned to his happy, safe home because I didn't belong in this paradigm. I was part of a different George's life, and that life had ended. It was for the best that I left, for the Henrys if not for me. I sensed the events of my trip to Willow Lane would haunt the remainder of my life, however short or long.

"I'm so happy for you and for George," I said.

And then the front door opened. My heart attempted to throw itself into my throat. I froze. Time again slipped free of its axis. Footsteps rose up from the landing.

Through the gaps in the wrought iron rail that delineated living room from stairs, I caught flashes of motion. Dark hair. Blue eyes. A

39

youthful face. The face of a ghost granted to one of the living.

George.

The dead-returned-to-life, a lost friend brought back by the lottery, rounded the rail. I'd forgotten how young George was the last time we were together, and it reminded me how old I was in my present.

"Hey," he said, and flashed a wary smile, a typical reaction from a teenaged boy uncomfortable in his own skin. Nerves, I sensed—not because he recognized me, but because I was an unfamiliar presence in his family's orderly house.

"Hello," I said, suddenly aware that my mouth had gone completely dry.

Our eyes briefly connected. A shiver tripped down my spine, curiously warmer than cold. When it passed, George was pecking a kiss onto his mother's cheek. This young man was also a gentleman, I thought. You get things right the second time around.

"Sweet ride out there," he said, his gaze again on me. "That car yours?"

"Yeah, that old heap's mine."

"Heap? She's a classic."

The ice broke somewhat. Mister Henry asked George about his schoolwork. Mrs. Henry introduced me by name. George extended his hand. I shook. My body was tempted to shiver again, but I willed it to steady.

"Honey, you should know . . . the two of you used to be friends," she said.

George's eyes sought mine. I detected a look, one I'm sure wasn't uncommon. It said I was from that other time, that other life, that

40

previous George.

"Oh, yeah," he said. "Thought you looked familiar. Figured it was because I saw you on TV."

I laughed for what felt the first time in ages.

I remembered the room with the blue wallpaper of sailing ships. Big ones, not mere sailboats. The kind that crossed vast and treacherous oceans. And the chess set with ceramic white and black pieces. It was a boy's dream bedroom, but to me it was also a snapshot frozen in time.

"I don't think it's any different," George said, his hands tucked into the tops of his pockets. He still looked nervous, though didn't struggle with word choices.

I didn't recall the previous version of my friend as being so well put together. "It's just like I remember."

"This must be weird for you," he said.

"Weirder for you, showing your room around to an old friend from high school you've never met. Emphasis on old."

"You into h-games? I've got 'Off-road Race' on holobox . . . but don't tell my folks. They're strange when it comes to anything involving cars. Understandable," George sighed.

"Sure is."

"They won't even let me drive by myself. I have my license."

I tipped a glance at the single bed with its heavy blue comforter, and exhaustion attempted to overwhelm me. My room at the hotel seemed light-years distant.

"Chess, maybe?" George asked.

I blinked myself out of the trance. "You don't remember me?"

41

He buried his eyes on the chessboard. "I didn't get his memories. That's not how it works, so they tell me. But there's something about you."

Tiny electric pinpricks rippled over my skin. "There is?"

"Yeah, maybe it's déjà vu. A feeling like I know you, or that I should."

There was so much I wanted to tell him, a lifetime's worth of apologies over what had happened. Worse, what hadn't. But to burden him with that kind of confession would be unfair. He was the Henrys' son, of that there was no doubt. But the young man was not my friend, my George Henry.

"Or, maybe you'll let me take that sweet ride of yours for a drive," he said. "I've never been up close to a car that classic!"

I caught the glint of mischief from his side of our bottled gaze. The same look, I imagined, that my George had shown whenever Al Packer pulled up to the curb in his Frankenstein assemblage of cobbled-together car parts.

"Your parents would boil me in oil."

"Then we won't tell them," George said.

I shook my head. "No."

He pleaded his case. "You're supposed to be my friend."

"I was—"

"Be my friend now. Let me take your car for a ride. I'll be with you, so it's safe. It won't be like before, with that other guy. Please."

I sat behind the wheel of my car, paralyzed on the outside, fighting a war with myself within. The white split-level with the crisp black shutters hovered at my back, a ghost visible whenever I tipped my eyes toward the rearview mirror.

Drive, the inner voice that had urged me to flee the Henrys' house again chimed in, attempting to get me away, back to the life I knew far from this neighborhood and town. Not much of a life. I worked as a line cook in a restaurant, lived in an apartment, not a real house, drove a third-world version of a car most people would be embarrassed to claim as their own—I was. My only claim to fame was a brief run in a lousy second-tier network h-TV show, and I'd fallen seven episodes short of winning the grand prize and bragging rights.

Drive. Forget you were here, that you even saw the second coming of George Henry.

I fell in reverse through time and memory, saw myself bobbing in our pool in the backyard of my family's long-abandoned house and swatting at a shuttlecock with a badminton racket in the Henrys'. And in these time-bytes, a young me and my George discussed the future.

"I'm going to be a famous restaurateur," that silly version of me boasted. "Write a series of best selling cookbooks. Have my own line of specialized cookware. Host TV shows, like all the great chefs."

"Maybe I'll race cars," said George.

Little did we know at the time that neither of us had a future.

Motion stirred in the rearview mirror, ripples of darkness set before the pristine white of the house. Footsteps sounded nearby. George appeared at the driver's side window. My palsy broke.

"I snuck out through the garage," he said, his voice barely above a whisper.

"I don't like this."

George leaned down. Through the open window, the spring

43

breeze stirred his scent of clean skin, toothpaste, a hint of deodorant. "You promised."

"I didn't."

"You want to be free of what happened. How do you think I feel? Imagine being me. How do I get over it when they never even let me behind the wheel of a car?"

Perhaps he was right. I didn't know. I was beyond thinking clearly. "Okay," I said, and slid over to the passenger's seat. "But not far."

"Just around the neighborhood," George said, and got in.

He turned the key in the ignition, adjusted the rearview, and threw my old gellet-guzzler into drive. Then he gunned the gas, and we tore away from the side of Willow Lane, kicking up lawn and gravel and leaving rubber on the pavement.

"Slow down," I said.

"I'm only going five above the limit. Stop being so parental."

I glanced over, saw his smile in the glow of houselights as we passed, and wanted to feel that young again, that hopeful. Only I knew better. I'd already lived through multiple lifetimes with George.

He fiddled with the radio.

"Stop that. Focus," I said.

He dismissed my remark with a sigh. A song by a band I hadn't heard since the first George died poured out of the satellite channel he selected—oldies. Ice chilled my blood. George drummed on the steering wheel in tune to the music. Houses and streetlamps flashed past. The car accelerated over the asphalt.

"You can't know what it's like," he said above the sad beat of the song's refrain. "Being me. Being him. I mean, which one of us got the soul?"

I blinked. The car rocketed forward. Beyond the windshield, the unmistakable crest of Barron Drive materialized. We were at the top of the hill, about to plummet down, down.

"George, no," I pleaded. "Slow down!"

I'd escaped the malevolent hunger of the maples at the bottom of that slope once earlier in the day, but doubted I would again, especially with George Henry in the car. They'd already sipped of his life force, had grown to monstrous proportions since their last feeding. We couldn't survive this. We wouldn't.

I looked to my left and, for an instant, the man behind the wheel was older. My age. A version of George from parallel time that had survived that ugly day; had lived to make a run at his dreams. Had, maybe, made them manifest.

We slipped out of the glow of one streetlamp and back into darkness. On the other side, the driver was again a teenage boy, traveling too fast over the speed limit, haunted by the specter of his own ghost.

The bottom dropped out of the world, and we spiraled toward the trees, toward death, toward—

George slammed on the brakes. For a terrible instant, gravity seized hold of our bodies and readied to hurl us through the windshield. Only this time, we were wearing our seatbelts. Tire treads gripped the dry road, and my old heap came to a complete stop, inches shy of the tree trunks.

I pulled up to the Henrys' place. A light was on in the living room. The rest of the house sat dark. Part of me longed to rest my head inside those walls, knowing I was safe and loved. But that wouldn't be for me. It was, though, his reality, and as he stepped out of the car, a strange emotion rose up from my guts. I felt happier than I could remember.

George leaned an elbow on the open window. "Sorry."

"Don't be. You've slain the demon. Now, you're free."

I scooted behind the wheel. I was free, too.

"Will you come back? We could hang out."

I told him I wasn't sure, but was fairly certain I wouldn't. I had exorcised the bad spirits of my past on Barron Drive.

"George," I said and, reaching up, cupped his chin. "Have the best future possible. Love your life."

He said he would. As I drove away, I believed him.

Food for Thought

What would it be like to meet a friend who had been dead for twenty years, brought back to life through a technological marvel like cloning? Would it be the same person? It seems strange to think they could be the same person in any meaningful sense. They lack the same life experiences that would seem to be key in determining who a person is. There is also the question of the soul. It would seem that if Aristotle was right and the soul is the form of the body, then they would both get a distinct soul, but perhaps it would be a problem under some other conception of the idea. What burdens and expectations would there be on such a person? To be the reincarnated version of someone else?

About the Author

Writer Gregory L. Norris grew up on a healthy dose of creature double features and classic Science Fiction TV. A former feature writer and columnist at *Sci Fi*, the official magazine of the Sci Fi Channel (before all those ridiculous Ys invaded), Norris once worked as a screenwriter on two episodes of Paramount's STAR TREK: VOYAGER series. He is the author of the handbook to all-things-Sunnydale, *The Q Guide to Buffy the Vampire Slayer*, and two paranormal romance novels offered as part of Home Shopping Network's "Escape With Romance" line—the first time HSN has offered novels to their global customers. In 2014, Norris was hired as screenwriter on two feature films, including the terrifying horror movie, *Brutal Colors* (releasing in First Quarter 2015). Twice, his short stories have notched "honorable mentions" in Ellen Datlow's *Year's Best* anthologies. Recent short story appearances include *Wicked Seasons, Anthology Year III* (the companion book to Anthocon, an annual conference for genre writers and readers), and *Enter at Your Own Risk: Dreamscapes into Darkness*, which also features reprints by Mary Shelley, Sir Arthur Conan Doyle, and Edgar Allen Poe. Norris lives in and writes from the mountains of New Hampshire, in a beautiful old New Englander house called Xanadu. His career has been featured numerous times in print interviews, on radio, and on television.

48

The Great Teacher

By Scott Chaddon

The first sensation Reed Logan registered was the cold, the second was the sound of hydraulics pushing open the canopy to his cryotube. Sitting up slowly, he looked around the pristine white control cabin. Swinging his legs over the edge, he cleared his throat and inhaled. The air was stale.

"Ginger?" he asked into the empty room.

"Good afternoon, Colonel Logan," a decidedly feminine voice replied. "How are you feeling?"

"You already know I'm in perfect health, Ginger," said Reed to the computer.

"Yes Colonel," replied Ginger. "It did, however, seem to be the polite thing to ask."

Logan nodded that it did.

"I need a status update please, Ginger," requested Logan. "Where, when, and why are we here, and what is the current situation?" A moment or two passed.

"I am in the process of downloading all stored communications

49

and doing an internal sensor sweep and ship-status scan. I will inform you as soon as relevant information is compiled. There is quite a bit, so it may take a few hours."

"Hours?" Reed sounded surprised. "I'll be interested to know how long I've been asleep." The trouble with cryosleep while traveling at relativistic speeds was that catching up with current events took a while and calculating exactly when you were in comparison to earth normal time took some doing. Even Ginger's advanced AI brain was challenged, so it must have been quite a while. "What can you tell me about where we are?"

"We have made planetfall in a previously unmapped yellow dwarf solar system and landed on its fourth planet. The planet has two medium-sized moons, is sixty percent covered with liquid water, the remaining forty percent is a single land mass containing plant and animal life of a wide variety. The atmosphere is rich in oxygen, nitrogen, and trace gasses. In short, Colonel, it is a Gaia planet. Perfect for our purposes."

"What purposes?" asked Reed, both curious and concerned. "What is the ship's status?"

"The ship suffered minor damage two months after take-off. An unregistered drone attempted to destroy us. The damage affected our ability to transmit back our updates and destroyed one of the raw material tanks. Sensors indicate a stray asteroid in the Oort Cloud we were moving through collided with the drone, destroying it.

We have landed to effect repairs, swap out water and air, and replenish supplies. All required materials and supplies are abundant and nearby. The ship's repair drones will gather the materials and begin correcting the damage as soon as its full extent has been ascertained.

We have landed because the systems could travel no further without effecting repair. Once repairs are complete we will begin to transmit our accumulated data back to Earth, where our vast store of galactic charts and data can be used for future travels."

Reed nodded as he absorbed this information. "So, Ginger, can you estimate how long until repairs, refueling and re-supply will be complete?"

"No more than three days Colonel," said the AI, "the planet appears to be safe. Any potential dangers would be easily managed by your nanites."

Nanites. Humanity's single greatest medical achievement and the source of its possessors' ultimate demise. Microscopic AI-driven machines introduced to a host that repair and replace any weak or damaged tissue. If tissue is no longer capable of being repaired, the nanites construct perfectly integrated cybernetics at the cellular level. The results make the possessor hard to damage, quick to heal, slow to age, stronger, faster and gives a near computer-like memory. Those were the benefits. It had been discovered that bioenergy was a fact, not a theory, and that a certain amount of living tissue was required to maintain one's humanity and, ultimately, one's life.

Reed was about twenty percent cyborg at this time and, fortune permitting, the nanites would allow him to reach just short of a thousand years old before he reached the ninety percent event horizon that turned him into a soulless automaton. When one hundred percent was reached, he would die and become a lifeless statue.

The nanites in Reed's body were developed as the Earth's sole uncorrupted science. There were, of course, commercial nanites but they, like all commercial products, were subject to built-in flaws, updates, upgrades, hacking, EMPs, break downs, rogue products, etc., so that the manufacturers could squeeze money out of the populace. By the time Colonel Logan had departed the Earth, nanites were required just to survive the ruined environments, and the populace worked itself to its enhanced bones just to pay for each upgrade that would ensure their survival.

Reed's nanites were different: their information on human anatomy, cell structure, nerve paths, repair, replication and replacement programs were hardwired into their tiny AIs and were complete and perfect. Tremendous effort had gone into the careful construction and uncorrupted programming of each nanite. Hundreds of billions of dollars created twelve nanites, one for each host. Once introduced, the single nanite would adapt itself perfectly to the host's genetic code, cell structure and physiology, then it would begin replication and the numbers would grow exponentially until nanites teemed in every part of the host's body —waiting to be useful in fighting damage, disease, fatigue and aging. Nanites were not interchangeable, and could not be given or transferred to another person. If a nanite found itself in a foreign system, it would shut down and self-destruct, eventually being flushed from the recipient's system, amid the rest of the waste.

Reed Logan's mission, and that of the eleven other mission members was to explore and reseed a more civilized human race on some distant world, untouched by the sins of the home world, and guided by the long-lived pilots in the ways of civilized peace and respect that Earth could not achieve. This thought prompted a question.

"Ginger, what is the status on the embryo bay?"

"Checking," said Ginger. "The embryo bay is completely gone Colonel. I'm sorry." Ginger's voice sounded truly sympathetic. The young in the bay were the primary mission. All stellar data being returned to earth was accurate except for any report of existing

Gaia worlds. The last thing that dying culture needed was a new place to spread to. Reed's heart sank. What was he doing out here if he couldn't bring life and happiness to a new world? He took some comfort that there were eleven others out there somewhere who could complete the mission where he could not.

After minutes of brooding turned into hours, Ginger spoke up.

"Colonel?" she asked.

"Yes Ginger," he answered.

"It's evening out and will be light for several hours yet. Perhaps you should take a walk and refresh yourself." The idea broke him out of his circular reverie.

"That sounds splendid Ginger," he said. "Thank you." He rose from where he was sitting and moved to a nearby control panel. A moment later a large display lit up, it divided into several sections, giving a decent view of the terrain on all sides of the small ship. A forest began a hundred meters to the east, a small lake to the north extended until it bordered the forest, a low set of rocky hills lay to the southwest and all the rest was fields and brush. In the greater distance to the north much larger mountains loomed, dark and without detail. The far edge of the lake held a curious glint along the water.

"Have our scouting drones reached the far side of the lake yet?" asked Reed.

"No Colonel," replied Ginger, "they have only gone as far as a kilometer, far enough to locate our necessary raw materials."

"I think I'll investigate," replied Reed. "You have my nanites' frequency Ginger?"

"Yes Colonel," she said. "Enjoy your trip."

"Thank you Ginger." Logan exited the control room, made his

way to the docking bay, lowered the ramp and exited the ship. Looking back at it he thought it looked, with its solar arrays extended, like a huge insect—maybe a mosquito—just standing on its narrow, jointed struts in the open field; glinting in the light of the westering sun.

Getting his bearings, he headed toward the edge of the lake that would take him to the glinting he could still just see. The nanites allowed him to travel without tiring or slowing, so he covered the distance quickly. As he approached, whatever reflective surface he was seeing at a distance became lost behind low hills. He crested the nearest hill, peering down into the valley. He stood, stunned by what he saw below him. People, human beings, an entire village of human beings filled the floor of the valley, surrounding a tributary stream that fed the lake.

"Ginger, are you seeing this?" asked Logan

"Clear as day Colonel," she replied. "I am at a loss, sir. I know of no colonization efforts this far out. We don't even have a name for this star, never mind its planets. Additionally, I doubt we were passed by a faster ship. This should not be possible."

"I'm going to proceed cautiously, but continue my exploration," said Reed.

"Of course, sir," said Ginger. "Signal is strong and the hills won't be an obstacle."

Reed strolled carefully down the hill, curiosity and wonder filling his heart and mind. Young men, women and children paused as he passed, smiled at him and continued on their way as though nothing strange had just wandered into their home. Every person he saw was either mostly or completely nude, treated one another with unveiled respect, concern and affection. Perfect harmony.

"Translator actively finding language patterns, sir," chimed in

Ginger. "We'll have you understanding and speaking the language in a few minutes, Colonel."

"Thank you Ginger," replied Logan as he continued to observe these remarkable people. They all seemed to be healthy and happy. While Ginger was still working on the translator, a young woman, not more than seventeen by his estimation, ran up, took his hand and started leading him into the village toward a strange pool of liquid that glowed brightly with a blue-white light. Curious, Logan followed and joined a circle of young people as they watched six young adults, Reed figured them to be about twenty-five years old. They made the circle, hugging and kissing each one in turn, even him, before taking positions just outside the pool. As one, they walked up and stepped into the glowing liquid. The six in the liquid began to glow as well, they became so bright that even Logan's nanite compensators in his eyes could not block it all out. When the light died down the six young adults were gone and the group began to dissipate and speak among themselves. Reed wasn't sure what it was he had just witnessed. As his focus returned, he noticed the young girl who had brought him was still standing nearby. Her lips were moving and slowly the words began to make sense.

"Translation matrix complete," reported Ginger in his ear.

". . . and so you do not need to feel confused. Do you understand?" said the girl.

"I'm not sure I do," said Reed. "Where did they go?"

"Ah, you understand me now," said the girl. "They have gone to cycle, the joyous re-beginning."

"I still don't know if I understand," replied Reed.

"The Father can explain better," said the girl with a smile. "Go speak with Father." Then she ran off and he watched her join a throng of other happy teenagers.

Reed proceeded toward what seemed to be the center of the community. Everyone he passed seemed to have a merry greeting for him and after a while the good sentiments were contagious. The center of town seemed to be a large playground where scores of small children played gleefully, watched only by a bent old man with a long gray beard, seated on a bench and leaning on a wooden stick, smiling and laughing. Something about the old man struck him as odd. He could not put his finger on it, so he circumnavigated the playground and continued to explore the town. Everywhere he went he experienced happy, accepting people.

As the sun dipped below the horizon and the first of the two moons rose, Reed was invited inside for a share of dinner. He wasn't concerned about possible toxins, the nanites would deal with anything harmful. So as they ate, he discovered that by decree of the father, no lifetime exceeded twenty five years of age. And for every sacrifice to the pool of light, a new baby was born and so the population remained stable, healthy, and happy. He discovered also that they look forward to going into the pool and do it voluntarily.

Just as dinner was being finished Reed's questions seemed to be going in circles. Why would they want to die? They would respond with, 'Why wouldn't you?' Just then Ginger cut in.

"Colonel?" her voice sounded troubled "Are you sitting down?" Reed actually tilted his head, perplexed, why would that be important?

"As a matter of fact," he replied, "I am. Report please."

"Sir, I have compiled the messages from Earth and the encrypted messages from the other eleven." Did her voice actually tremble?

"And . . ." prompted Reed

"We are alone sir," she almost whispered.

"Of course we're alone," he said. "We lost the embryo bay."

"No . . .," she said. "You don't understand."

"Then explain, Ginger," he said, feeling mildly troubled now.

"I have calculated our current time frame, Colonel," she started.

"When are we, Ginger?" Reed prompted.

"It is the year 6379 by Earth reckoning," reported Ginger.

"What?" Reed almost yelled aloud. "Twenty-five hundred years?"

"That is correct, sir," confirmed the AI.

"What do all the reports say?" asked Logan "What is happening on Earth now?"

"Nothing," she almost whispered. "Absolutely nothing, sir."

"Explain." Reed felt a drop of acid fear strike his heart. All the talking at the table stopped, and everyone looked at him with sympathy.

"Approximately a thousand years ago," she said "Earth died, sir, and everyone on it as well."

"All dead?" he whispered. "What happened?"

"The faulty nanites had a community cascade effect and they all failed. The environment did the rest," she reported.

"What about the other eleven?" Desperate hope seeped into his voice, even as grief attempted to rob him of it.

"All dead sir," She stated. "The drone that damaged us had brothers that succeeded where ours failed. Some kind of espionage by a terrorist faction. Some tried escaping in ships only to be turned back by our nearest neighboring alien civilizations. They prevented any evacuation."

"I can't really blame them," shrugged Reed as he began to be consumed by grief and pain. He was the last of his kind. Hands

57

touched him, startling him out of his pain. Concerned, pained faces surrounded him, he felt their compassion and caring. And their presence and companionship helped.

Wait, thought Reed to himself, everyone here is human. Somehow we survived. After his mind was swamped with grief, he felt a need to sleep. Confused, he asked Ginger about being tired.

"Emotional exhaustion," she said "is different than physical exhaustion. You need to sleep, sir, for your own good."

He was led to a room with a soft bed. He didn't lay down right away, the nervous energy and tension, mixed with survivor's guilt and grief kept him awake. Sweet and sour memories conflicted in his mind and denied him rest. The details of the demise of his culture and race would be waiting on the ship for him to review at his leisure, right now he was thunderstruck. Instead of relaxing, his stress levels were spiraling upward, approaching dangerous levels. A warning indicator shimmered into view, went from yellow and moved quickly into red. Reed ignored it, though in the back of his mind he knew what was going to happen. Clutching his head, as he wept and paced the floor, he was in mid-stride when everything went black.

It was well past midday when he awoke and wondered how he had gotten into the bed; his grief and solitude were softened slightly by the presence of the natives here. After the sixth person he encountered told him that he should probably go talk to Father he gradually decided that he probably should find out who this "Father" was, exactly. The sharp edge of his grief over the loss of his species was significantly dulled by the constant presence of the clearly human population here. He found it increasingly difficult to grieve for a planet that ultimately destroyed itself through its own greed and inhumane treatment of itself. Still, the loss of everything he ever knew continued to sting him deeply; it was a difficult concept to wrap his mind around, the loss of everything.

At first he wandered through the city, almost aimlessly, always seeming to be drawn back towards the playground. In his haze of pain and solitude, he stood numbly and watched the small children play happily with one another on the equipment. Ginger had performed full scans and reported to him that these were indeed fully human people, not clones, not androids, not extraterrestrial doppelgangers, but human—all the way down to the cellular and genetic levels. Just below his pain lay his curiosity. How? How could they be here? With Earth a thousand years dead and cold. Parallel, identical evolution was a statistical impossibility. Yet here they were, healthy and happy and thriving? How?

As always the old man sat and watched the children, delighted in their innocent joy and play. Reed stood and stared for what seemed like hours when a single point of strangeness pierced his self-generated gloom. This was the only person older than twenty-five he had seen anywhere in this entire city. Wrinkled skin, long, gray hair, thin, mildly arthritic fingers with a pleasant smile on his face and in his eyes. After a moment of recognition, the old man gestured for Reed to have a seat on the bench beside him. Carefully Reed sat down and watched the old man.

"Are you the one the people here call 'Father'?" asked Reed finally. The old man watched Reed for only a moment, though it seemed as though the man looked right through him and into the deepest parts of his being. The old man nodded.

"Yes," he said softly. "I am."

"May I ask you a few questions?" asked Reed

"Of course," nodded Father.

"Why do they all call you 'Father'?" said Reed. There was a momentary pause.

"Why do you call a tree, a tree?" responded Father "Or a rock, a rock? It is what it means to you. To them I am Father and so that is what I am." The answer was as clear as it was ambiguous. Reed wasn't sure what to quite make of it.

"If I may, sir," began Reed. "Why is there no one here, except you, any older than twenty-five? And how can they be happy with such a short life span? To go so joyfully to their deaths?"

"Theirs is the age of happiness," stated Father. "Much beyond that and the mind corrupts the heart, and that is the first step on the path to destruction. They are happy because they get to begin again, reborn on that very day. They keep their knowledge and memories but are given new innocence and freedom, the burden of years is lifted."

"So, there is no progress here?" wondered the Colonel. "A stagnant culture?"

"No..." replied the old man. "All you see was built by these people. They progress carefully and wisely, their wisdom preserved through each life. They do not waste nor do they act against one another. Instead, they act to benefit all."

That struck Reed as strange, not at all the human behavior he was familiar with. In fact, it was contrary to most of humanity as he knew it.

"That isn't normal human behavior, as I know it, Father," said Reed, echoing his thoughts. "Why are they so unselfish and caring, supportive and giving?"

"They are all highly sensitive empaths," he replied. "More so even than you. Any slight they cause, any harm at all, and they all know who is hurting and who did the hurting and it is corrected so all may be happy. There are no secrets here."

The phenomenon of empathic psionic ability had been proven

and documented long ago, but true empaths had died out on Earth long before his time, unable to handle the turmoil, deception, cruelty and barbarism of the culture. But an entire culture of true empaths would be remarkable, and make good sense, too.

"I wish my culture had been able to achieve this." Reed gestured around.

"Your culture was different Reed," said Father. Reed turned suddenly, surprised at this comment. Before he could say anything the old man continued. "Your people were created to be creators, not sensitives, you were given choices and made to live with them and the consequences. Allowed to evolve and explore on your own, to be watched and observed. What does your culture tell you that the greatest teacher is?"

This question momentarily derailed his own line of questions, as Reed considered the various possible answers.

"Failure," responded Reed. "Failure is the greatest of teachers. We learn a lot more from a single failure than we do from a hundred easy successes. Excuse me sir, but how do you know my culture? How do you know my name?" He had not been asked, nor had he given anyone his name since he awakened on board. Perhaps the old man was a telepath.

"You may take your rest here, Reed," said Father "There is nothing human beyond this point, but you are welcome to look if you so choose. They will call you 'Uncle' for the long duration of your life and they will love you and revere you. When your time has come you may enter the pool and be reborn into this culture, retaining as they do, all of your knowledge but regaining your innocence and happiness."

"Who are you?" asked Reed, now bewildered.

"I am the Father, Reed," said the old man. "And I am truly sorry for your pain." A single, glittering tear ran slowly from his eye and down his cheek. "Perhaps you could learn to forgive me some day."

"Forgive you?" asked Reed quietly. "For what?" The old man looked into Reed's eyes for the first time. The depths of those eyes were unfathomable, galaxies and universes glittered in the depths, creation, time and immortality only accents. All creation was hidden behind those eyes.

"Even a God must learn from its mistakes." The tear fell, glittering, from his face.

Food for Thought

Would you take the nanite treatment that would extend your life but inevitably turn you into an automaton and eventually kill you? Would you volunteer to be the god walking with a new Adam and Eve in a new Eden? Leading and guiding your charges in their new world? How would you cope with learning that you were the last of your kind?

What do you make of the lesson of the story? That failure is the greatest teacher, that success is something that can happen at the end of a series of failures and missteps?

About the Author

Scott Chaddon is 47 and was born and raised in Fairbanks, Alaska. He attended the University of Alaska, Fairbanks, earning a Bachelor's in Art, with a Minor in Theatre. As an artist, he paints, draws, sculpts, does metal working, and has had showings in Fairbanks, AK. Recently, at the encouragement of his wife, he began submitting his writing for publication, and has had six pieces accepted. He has two children, and three wonderful grandsons.

Scott presently lives with his wife of seven years on a farm in Missouri, with a small menagerie of animals- including chickens, rabbits, dogs, and cats.

2016 marks the 50th anniversary from the launch of Star Trek: The Original Series. To commemorate such an event, the organisers are planning the second Star Trek Symposium.

This will differ from the traditional Fan-Based Convention in that it will be a platform for academics from across many disciplines to meet and explore this particular intersection between the Humanities and the Sciences.

The first Star Trek Symposium held in 2014 was well received, thus motivating the organizers to celebrate Star Trek's Golden Anniversary with this second event.

The Symposium will be held under the auspices of HUMS, the Humanities, Medicine and Sciences Programme at the University of Malta. The Star Trek Symposium will appeal to both scientists and fans of science fiction. Come and join us in Malta!

Web: www.startreksymposium.com
Email: info@startreksymposium.com

Articles

Civic Militarism and Heinlein's "Starship Troopers"

Patrick S. Baker

Civic Militarism and Western History

Civic militarism is the idea that active citizenship is a transactional relationship between the nation and its citizens. In short, the concept is that a free citizen joins in the military forces of their country and fights to defend it, and in return the citizen is recognized as a fully participating member of the body politic, with all the rights and obligations attendant to that position. Also civic militarism, at least in the West, acknowledges that even when joining the military, people retain most of their civil and human rights. Historically, nation-states with a high level of civic militarism have favored civilian control of the military, citizen militias over professional armies and conscription in times of need.[4]

---

[4]Patrick G Skelly, "Evolution in 'The Western Way of War': Continuity, Punctuated Equilibrium, Neither?" (Norwich University, School of Graduate Studies, Master of Arts in Military History) 28 May 2006 online at http://www.milhist.net/norwich/pskelly2.pdf.; Victor Davis Hanson, "War and the West, Then and Now", paper presented at

In the West, civic militarism developed from the ancient Greeks. The citizen body of the democratic city-states would vote for a war, then march out to fight in that war. It is not too much to say that the average Greek citizen thought of himself as a defender of his city-state first. For example, the Athenian tragic playwright Aeschylus' epitaph read: "Beneath this stone lies Aeschylus, son of Euphorion, the Athenian, who perished in the wheat-bearing land of Gela; of his noble prowess the grove of Marathon can speak, or the long-haired Persian who knows it well." Not even a mention of his plays, just that he fought the Persians at the Battle of Marathon.[5]

As Machiavelli stated in "The Prince": "The principle foundations of all states... are good laws and good armies. And because there cannot be good laws where armies are not good, and where there are good armies, there must be good laws... that the arms with which a prince defends his state are either his own, or they are mercenaries, auxiliaries, or mixed. Mercenaries and auxiliaries are useless and dangerous," so, "The wise prince, therefore, has always avoided these [mercenary] arms and turned to his own..."[6]

---

the University of Oregon, 11 February 2004, Part One, online at http://victorhanson.com/

[5]Rosalie F. Baker and Charles F. Baker III, "Ancient Greeks: Creating the Classical Tradition" (Oxford: Oxford University Press, 1997), 54.

About 130 years after Machiavelli's "The Prince" was published, Jean-Jacques Rousseau proposed in his "Considerations on the Government of Poland and on its Proposed Reformation" that the only proper army for a free state was a citizen army: "Each citizen should be a soldier by duty... Such was the military system of the Romans; such is that of the Swiss today; such ought to be that of every free state... A good militia, a genuine, well-drilled militia, is alone capable of satisfying this need."[7]

In Continental Europe, civic militarism was top-down driven, with governments requiring service from their citizens in the form of conscription and devoting large parts of the economy to the military effort, creating a so-called "nation at arms." This idea is exemplified by the French National Convention's levee-en-masse edict of 1793: "From this moment... all Frenchmen are in permanent requisition for the services of the armies. The young men shall fight; the married men shall forge arms and transport provisions; the women shall make tents and clothes and shall serve in the hospitals; the children shall turn old lint into linen; the old men shall betake themselves to the public squares in order to arouse the courage of the warriors and preach hatred of kings and the unity of the Republic."[8]

---

[6]Niccolo Machiavelli, "The Prince", (1532), Chap. 12 and 13.

[7]Jean-Jacques Rousseau, "Considerations on the Government of Poland and on its Proposed Reformation" (1772), Chapter XII.

In the 19th and 20th Centuries, mass conscription and the ability to rapidly grow huge armies was the mark of a nation with a strong concept of civic militarism and an active citizen population. For example, during the four years of the First World War, Britain's army grew from just 250,000 men to over 5.7 million through a combination of active recruiting and conscription. Another example is the American army in World War Two, which grew from a mere 190,000 men in 1939 to over 12 million by 1945. At this time, people did not surrender most of their rights by joining the military. Rights to property, rights against self-incrimination, trial by jury, legal representation, and redress of grievances were all still in place for service members. On discharge a veteran received generous benefits: pensions, loan guarantees for home and businesses, access to and money for education, medical care for service related injuries, etc. [9]

---

[8]French National Convention, "Levee en masse edict", (23 August 1793).

[9]Ian Beckett, "The Nation in Arms (1914 – 1918)" in *A Nation in Arms,* ed. Ian F W Beckett and Keith Simpson (Barnsley, UK: Pen and Sword, Ltd., 1985), 2-15; Geoffrey Perret, "There's a War to be Won: The United States Army in World War Two", (New York: Ballentine Books, 1991), 27 and 465; United States V. Tempia, 16 U.S.M.C.A., 629, 37 C.M.R. 249 (1967); Lawrence J. and Katrina L. Webber, "The Complete Idiot's Guide to Your Military and Veterans Benefits", (New York: Alpha Books, 2008), 268-269.

Soldiers and Citizens

Throughout Western history, civic militarism was the armed support of democratic-republicanism. Democratic-republicanism is the stated belief that the best organization for a society is one, "... composed of a body of self-governing citizens whose primary duty is to defend their republic." Further, historically, "martial values were cultivated... not only because they were needed to defend the city, but also because they were highly valued in themselves as a main source of citizen virtue and loyalty."[10]

It is the concept that "martial values" are the main source of "citizen virtue" that Robert A. Heinlein in his 1959 Hugo Award-winning novel "Starship Troopers" proposed the idea that only those people that have served society in some manner should be allowed to be full citizens. That is to say, only people that have completed some variety of, "Federal Service of the Terran Federation," may vote, hold public office and join the civil service. Of course, this concept, the so-called "Heinlein Rule", has resulted in howls that the very notion is fascist, racist, sexist, elitist, and is militaristically authoritarian.[11]

---

[10]Doyne Dawson, "The Origins of Western Warfare: Militarism and Morality in the Ancient World", (Boulder, CO: Westview Press, 1996), 4.

[11]Robert Heinlein, "Starship Troopers" (New York: Ace Science Fiction, 1959/1990), 25, 27, 71 and 99; Brian Baker, "Science Fiction: A Readers' Guide to Essential Criticism" (London; Palgrave, 2014), 99.

Let us deal with each of these points in turn. First, is the "Heinlein Rule" fascistic?

Merriam-Webster defines fascism as, "a way of organizing a society in which a government ruled by a dictator controls the lives of the people and in which people are not allowed to disagree with the government." In no way is the Terran Federation a dictatorship. "Broadly drawn, [it] is a liberal, representative democracy. All residents are protected and enjoy the same legal rights as citizens...", except only citizens vote and hold political office. For example, the main character's father states, "a taxpayer has some rights," and the doctor examining newly joined members of the federal service talks about free speech. Another character states that in the Terran Federation, "... personal freedom for all is the greatest in history, laws are few, taxes are low, living standards are high... crime is at its lowest ebb." [12]

Is the concept racist and sexist? No. "Citizenship is open to all, regardless of race, creed, religion, gender or handicap." But it may only be obtained by, "demonstrated service to the state." Although Heinlein gives very little in the way of physical description of his characters, based on last names alone, the Federal Service is multi-ethnic. Ship's Sergeant Jelal is described as, "a Finno-Turk from Iskander around Proxima - a swarthy little

---

[12]Everett Carl Dolman, "Military, Democracy, and the State in Robert A. Heinlein's 'Starship Troopers'" in "Political Science Fiction" ed. by Donald M. Hassler and Clyde Wilcox (Columbia, SC: South Carolina University Press, 1997), 197. Heinlein, "Starship Troopers", 18, 24 and 143.

man..." Before combat the chaplain (who also fights) offers blessings to "Moslems, Christians, Gnostics, Jews, whoever..." In basic training, recruits show up unable to speak English and come from Germany, Japan, the American South and the Philippines. Character's last names include Spieksma, Mahmud, Zim, Chandar and Bearpaw. Further, the main character, Rico, is a Filipino whose native language is Tagalog. While women are excluded from the Army's combat arms, they serve in other branches, 40% of the Federal Service personnel assigned to Sanctuary Base are female. Also women are considered the best pilots, "their reactions are faster, and they can tolerate more gee," than men. Rico considers his friend Carmen, who is a pilot, to be a fellow "officer and a fighting man – as well as a very pretty girl."[13]

Is the idea elitist? No again. First: "the practice of accepting any and all residents into the Federal service (hence into citizenship) blunts the formation of an elitist social order..." Also, the Federal Service is amazingly equalitarian; there is no elite military academy, or even college-level Reserve Officer Training Course for the Army. An officer candidate, "must be a trained trooper, blooded under fire, a veteran of combat drops." Also in some places in the Federation, veterans are a vast majority of the population, up to 80 percent on one planet. Lastly, the idea that veterans are "picked" and "smarter" than other people is derided as "preposterous".[14]

Is the "Heinlein Rule" militaristically authoritarian? Far from

---

[13]Dolman, "Military, Democracy, and the State", 197; Heinlein, "Starship Troopers", 1, 3, 4, 34-36, 57, 124, 137, 138, 202 and 203.

it. The Terran Federation is very much a "law and order" society with an ascending schedule of harsh punishments for criminals, public floggings being the most common. Even minor offenses in the military may earn a soldier up to five lashes as, "administrative punishment." Also, the Federation has a comparatively large number of capital crimes: murder, kidnapping, demand for ransom and criminal neglect are mentioned as examples. But, both civilians and military members are subjected to the same set of laws, excepting those required to maintain military discipline, "the 31 Crash Landings." Trial by jury and trial by court martial, the right against self-incrimination and right to counsel are afforded the accused. Military jurisdiction only takes precedence over the civil law in the case of military members. Most importantly, active duty personnel are prohibited from voting.[15]

Further, Federal service is not strictly, or even largely, military. Heinlein says, "In 'Starship Troopers' it is stated flatly and more than once that nineteen out of twenty veterans are not military veterans. Instead, 95% of voters are what we call today 'former members of federal civil service'." Within the novel itself, a number of dangerous, but non-military positions, are listed, such as "terranizing Venus," "digging tunnels on Luna," and "field testing survival equipment on Titan." One character states, "In

---

[14]Dolman, "Military, Democracy, and the State", 210, Heinlein, "Starship Troopers", 141 – 143 and 150

[15]Ibid., 56, 83, 86 , 87, 142.

74

peacetime most veterans come from non-combat auxiliary services and have not been subjected to the full rigors of military discipline." However, the numbers mentioned by Heinlein in the quote are, in fact, not stated in the novel.[16]

While the Federal service seems authoritarian in theory, it is surprisingly forgiving in practice. Rico is involved in a bar brawl while on Rest and Recreation (R & R), and suffers no more punishment than having to pay for the broken furniture. In the Army, a soldier, "can quit thirty seconds before a drop... and all that happens is he is paid off and can never vote." [17]

One last point on the "Heinlein Rule" being militaristically authoritarian: Historically most, if not all authoritarian, as well as many non-authoritarian, societies have instituted military conscription as a way to impose a high level of societal discipline on their populations. This is not the case with the Terran Federation. Heinlein himself despised the military draft, saying it was nothing but "slavery". The Federal service is all volunteers and does not want draftees. Rico calls conscripts, "ersatz soldiers," and he'd rather have no one next to him than, "an alleged soldier who is nursing the 'conscript' syndrome."[18]

---

[16]Robert A. Heinlein, "Expanded Universe", (Riverdale, NY: Baen Books, 1980/2003), 325; Heinlein, "Starship Troopers", 23, 27, 142.

[17]Ibid., 124, 162.

[18]Thomas Hippler, "Citizens, Soldiers and National Armies:

Conclusion

The "Heinlein Rule" takes the idea of civic militarism to its logical conclusion. That is to say, only those people that have committed themselves to the service and defense of the state should and may have a say in how such a nation is organized and run. In this way, no one has social responsibility thrust on them by mere accident of birth, but rather must seek such responsibility by an act of free will, and responsibility which "requires imagination - devotion, loyalty, all the higher virtues."[19]

Bibliography

Baker, Rosalie F. and Charles F. Baker III, *Ancient Greeks: Creating the Classical Tradition*

Oxford: Oxford University Press, 1997.

Beckett, Ian. "The Nation in Arms (1914 – 1918)" in "A Nation in Arms." Edited Ian F. W.

Beckett and Keith Simpson, 1-37. Barnsley, UK: Pen and Sword, Ltd., 1985.

Military Service in France and Germany 1789 – 1830", (New York: Routledge, 2008), 1-4. Robert A. Heinlein, "Guest of Honor Speech at the XIXth World Science Fiction Convention in Seattle, 1961" in "Requiem: Collected Works and Tributes to the Grand Master" ed. Yoji Kondo (New York: Tor Books, 1992), 185; Heinlein, "Starship Troopers", 86.

[19]Heinlein, "Starship Troopers", 145.

Dawson, Doyne, *The Origins of Western Warfare: Militarism and Morality in the Ancient World*

Boulder, CO: Westview Press, 1996.

Dolman, Everett Carl. "Military, Democracy, and the State in Robert A. Heinlein's 'Starship

Troopers'" in "Political Science Fiction". Edited by Donald M. Hassler and Clyde Wilcox. 196-213. Columbia, SC: South Carolina University Press, 1997.

French National Convention, *Levee en masse edict.* 23 August 1793.

Hanson, Victor Davis. "War and the West, Then and Now", paper presented at the University of

Oregon. 11February 2004 online at http://www.victorhanson.com/

Heinlein, Robert. "Starship Troopers". New York: Ace Science Fiction, 1959/1990.

_____. "Guest of Honor Speech at the XIXth World Science Fiction Convention in Seattle,

1961." in "Requiem: Collected Works and Tributes to the Grand Master." 168-197. Edited by Yoji Kondo. New York: Tor Books, 1992.

_____. "Expanded Universe." Riverdale, NY: Baen Books, 1980/2003.

Hippler, Thomas. "Citizens, Soldiers and National Armies: Military Service in France and

Germany 1789 – 1830." New York: Routledge, 2008.

Machiavelli, Niccolò. *The Prince*. 1532

Perret, Geoffrey. *There's a War to be Won: The United States Army in World War Two*, New

York: Ballentine Books, 1991.

Rousseau, Jean-Jacques. *Considerations on the Government of Poland and on its Proposed*

Reformation. 1772

Skelly, Patrick G. "Evolution in 'The Western Way of War': Continuity, Punctuated Equilibrium,

Neither?" Norwich University, School of Graduate Studies, Master of Arts in Military History. 28 May 2006 online at http://www.milhist.net/norwich/pskelly2.pdf.

Webber, Lawrence J. and Katrina L. *The Complete Idiot's Guide to Your Military and*

Veterans Benefits. New York: Alpha Books, 2008.

United States V. Tempia, 16 U.S.M.C.A., 629, 37 C.M.R. 249. 1967.

About the Author

Patrick S. Baker is a U.S. Army Field Artillery Veteran, currently a Department of Defense employee. He holds Bachelor degrees in History and Political Science from the University of Missouri and a Masters in European History from American Military University. He is a part-time writer and military historian. His non-fiction work has appeared in Armchair General online, the Saber and Scroll Journal, Medieval and Ancient Warfare Magazines. His fiction has appeared in New Realms Magazine. In his spare time he reads, works-out, plays war-games and enjoys life with his wife, dog and two cats. His website is: https://bakerp2004.wordpress.com/

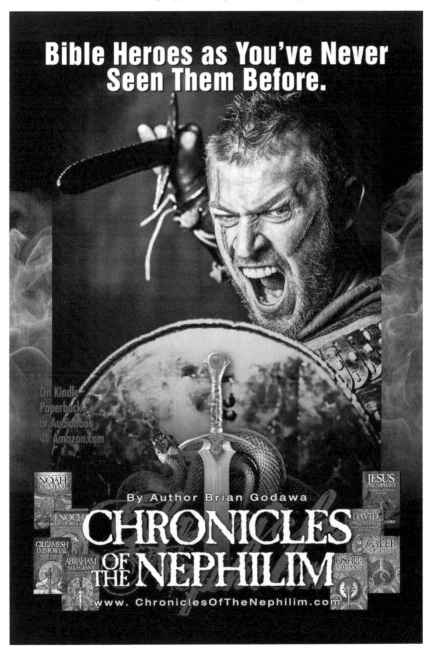

On Emotion Drugs

Jeffrey A. Corkern

Why are emotion drugs illegal?

Our society, in fact, all stable, functioning societies in the world, do NOT like emotion drugs for some strange reason. Emotion drugs are drugs like pot, cocaine, heroin, LSD, meth, Ecstasy and so forth. They spend literally HUNDREDS of billions of dollars fighting emotion drugs. "War On Drugs" is not an over-exaggeration to describe this worldwide effort, not in the least. The expenditure easily matches what has been spent on fighting real shooting wars.

This world's societies are SERIOUS about this war. A lot of this world's societies will stand you up against a wall and SHOOT YOU DEAD if they catch you selling emotion drugs. You wanna know the weirdest thing? The world's societies can't really tell you WHY they're doing this.

They can't answer the question of why they're making this EXTREME effort against emotion drugs. They can't. Not one society in this world can give an answer to that question that you can't shoot down with the greatest of ease. If they could give an entirely logical answer, an answer that could convince EVERYBODY that emotion drugs really were intrinsically bad things, an argument everybody could understand, they wouldn't be having such a hard time keeping people away from emotion drugs. They wouldn't be having to spend so much money.

This extreme effort seems strange to a lot of people. So much so there are organizations---like NORML, the National Organization to Reform the Marijuana Laws, for example, and many others, that are actively trying to make emotion drugs legal.

One sign of everyone's complete and total confusion is they haven't even correctly labeled these things as what they are, EMOTION drugs, that is. Drugs that make people feel good, that MAKE people feel a certain EMOTION they want to feel.

Let's run through a couple of these worthless arguments against emotion drugs and shoot them down, just to illustrate how completely and totally confused this anti-emotion-drug thing is. The first objection you hear is that it's wrong to use emotion drugs because they're illegal. Right. This is so astoundingly illogical it takes your breath away. An example of circular logic at its finest. Because they're illegal? Easily cured, man. Just make the damn emotion drugs legal. Then it'll be right. Just make all emotion drugs legal and let corporations sell them just like soda pop. You'll save how many HUNDREDS of billions of dollars? How much drug crime will go away? How many prisons will be COMPLETELY emptied? How much money will you rake in on taxes? It'll be in the billions! You'll make every nickel back you spent on that futile War on Drugs! People will spend money on emotion drugs before they'll spend money on FOOD, man!

Which brings up the second objection. Emotion drugs in general hurt their users. Letting people use emotion drugs will be allowing people to damage themselves, even kill themselves. Several of these emotion drugs will kill you deader than a hammer if you slip just one little inch. First answer to that: There are quite a number of activities that people do in this world that are just as dangerous (or MORE!), that can kill you just as dead, and none of the world's societies forbid these activities. Things like sky-diving, high-speed auto racing, airplane racing, hang-gliding, scuba diving and mountain climbing. If you slip just one little inch doing any of these activities or any of a thousand other risky activities—you're DEAD, quicker than a heartbeat.

You know, it's odd, but we can abstract a rule from this observed behavior. We can abstract a single, simple rule the world's societies are using to determine what is and is NOT allowed behavior to get happy. You can do anything you want that doesn't hurt other people to get happy except stimulate the happiness centers of your brain directly. Anything else is allowed, even if you can get yourself killed doing it. Somehow death doesn't matter. Indirect stimulation of your brain's happiness centers is legal. Direct stimulation of your brain's happiness centers is NOT.

Second answer to that: Okay, so what if we find a way of stimulating the brain's happiness centers that DOESN'T hurt the user? That has no side-effects and is not physically addicting and impossible to overdose on. The perfect drug or class of emotion drugs. Then we can make that one class of emotion drugs alone legal. Impossible to make a single chemical that does that, you say? Chemicals ALWAYS have side-effects. Well, actually, you're probably right, if you're talking about chemical substances.

Fortunately, science is marching on. The human race is no longer restricted to chemical substances when it comes to getting stoned, pardon me, happy. We can cut right to the chase these days, without having to use any kind of nasty chemicals with their nasty side effects, with direct electrical brain stimulation. We can run a little metal wire right to certain sections of your brain, trickle a few milliamps of current to it and you will be in Nirvana INSTANTLY, man, higher than a kite with NO side-effects. The groundwork has already been laid. Neuroscientists have ALREADY discovered precisely what sections of brain to tickle, believe it or not.

So there we have it, the perfect happiness drug. Or machine, rather. So now all objections to emotion drugs have been refuted. So now we can make all emotion drugs and machines legal. Right?

Right! There's not a single objection we can't shoot down. We can't find a single truly logical reason not to. W-e-l-l, perhaps not. Perhaps there are one or two teeny-tiny little objections to making emotion drugs, or machines, legal.

Let us examine this question as precisely as possible. (Which is something, by the way, the world's societies have NEVER done. They have just been reacting instinctively, stumbling around blind in the dark, on this subject.) First, let us define precisely what an emotion drug is. An "emotion drug" is a substance that is capable of directly affecting the emotion centers of the user's brain and is employed by the user for the SOLE purpose of affecting the emotion centers of his brain, for directly altering his emotional state.

Note that this definition is totally a use definition, i.e. the user is the one who defines what an emotion drug is. Let me illustrate what I mean. Smoking marijuana for the SOLE purpose of getting high defines marijuana as an emotion drug (and illegal). Smoking marijuana to, let us say, relieve the pain of menstrual cramps or to stimulate your appetite because anti-cancer drugs have suppressed your appetite defines marijuana as NOT an emotion drug (and legal). It is the purpose the user has for the drug that primarily determines whether or not the drug is an emotion drug. If it DIRECTLY affects his brain's emotion centers, it's an emotion drug. Anything else, it's not.

So now we have a working definition of "emotion drug." Which is also hereby defined to include, not just drugs, but also mechanical devices. Now, what rational, logical objection can we find to making these things legal? What do emotion drugs do?

Hmmmm. They make people happy. Fundamentally, the rock-bottom, that's what they do. They make people feel good. How in the world could that be a bad thing? I mean, everything else people do has as its sole purpose to get happy. Why aren't emotion drugs just another pathway to this emotional state?

Perhaps we should pause here a minute and look at this getting-happy thing. There is something quite astonishing about this getting-happy thing. You know why people do what they do? BECAUSE THEY'RE ALL TRYING TO GET HAPPY! You know what? You can describe ALL human action in terms of getting happy! No matter how small or how large, it's ALL about being happy! All of it, man! ALL OF IT!

You race cars at high speed because you enjoy it. You parachute out of perfectly good airplanes because it's fun. You play video games because it brings a smile to your face.

It goes deeper than that. A LOT deeper. You even BREATHE to stay happy, right? How happy are you going to feel if you STOPPED breathing? You get married, because being with that special other person makes you happier than anything else in this world.

You wanna know where this deep insight into human motivation first began to pop to the surface? To become consciously known? In the eighteenth century! In the eighteenth century, there was a great deal of philosophical inquiry into why people did what they did. And the answer they came up with was people did what they did in order to get happy. This was NOT just some airy-fairy philosophical conclusion, either. This conclusion GOT USED AS A FOUNDATION RULE FOR ONE OF THE WORLD'S MOST SUCCESSFUL SOCIETIES! Guess which one. The United States!

What does it say in the Declaration of Independence? "... life, liberty, and THE PURSUIT OF HAPPINESS!" The Founding Fathers were trying to lay the foundations for a successful society using this radical new discovery. And they did it, man, they did it. They absolutely NAILED it! Because ALL human action truly can be described as an effort to get happy! Smart guys, our Founding Fathers.

You have a family because it makes you happy. You get up every morning, go out and work like a damn dog because having a family, in the end, makes you happy, so happy you don't mind the extreme effort it takes. Whatever you do, it's to feel happiness in one form or another. It's all about being happy, your own personal happiness, and everybody else's, in the end.

Unless, of course, you use emotion drugs to get happy. Now you no longer need to do any of those other things. Now all you need is the emotion drug, a bag of pot, a line of coke, a wire to the brain. Now you don't need any of those other things to get happy anymore. Race cars, airplanes, video games, you don't need them, and something far more terrible you're not going to need.

You want to know what the most terrible thing is you're not going to need? You're not going to need other people. You're not gonna need other people, man. You can see this already happening in society. This is a known psychological effect of emotion drugs. Look at the people you know who use dope. Look at them REAL HARD. Are they not ISOLATED? Fundamentally cut off from the rest of the world? In a kind of unchanging stasis? Not going anywhere?

They don't HAVE to change, you see. With people who don't use emotion drugs, if they are in pain somehow and not happy, they are FORCED to change something about themselves or their environment in order to be happy. They are FORCED TO GET SMARTER about the Universe, to strike rock-bottom. This is NOT true for people who use emotion drugs. If they feel bad, they just go running to the dope, and PRESTO! They're happy! Without having to go through the effort of making all that nasty, wrenching, painful change of having to learn anything, of having to get smarter even the least little bit!

So they DON'T change or get smarter, and this is a known psychological effect of emotion drugs. If somebody started using emotion drugs at fifteen, you can examine him psychologically ten, twenty, thirty, forty years later and he will STILL be fifteen years old on the inside. He (or she, of course) will know what he knew at fifteen and NOTHING else.

You can see this same isolating effect in drug-related violent crime, too. Crimes committed while under the influence of emotion drugs have a tendency to be more violent. The emotion drugs have cut the criminal's emotional connection to the rest of humanity, you see, and the result is he does more horrible things to his victims than he would have had he not been under the influence.

Emotion drugs cut you off from EVERYTHING. Period. WITHOUT emotion drugs, you must interact with the world in order to get happy. WITH emotion drugs, you DON'T. Right?

You know what the definition of society is? People interacting with other people. What do emotion drugs do? Shut down that interaction with other people. With everything else, too, but primarily with other people.

So, if a society makes emotion drugs legal, what, inevitably, must legal emotion drugs do to that society in the end? DESTROY IT UTTERLY. Oopsie. NOW we have a rational, logical reason for a society to make emotion drugs illegal, VIOLENTLY illegal, put-you-in-jail-for-twenty-years illegal, stand-you-up-against-a-wall-and-SHOOT-YOU-DEAD illegal. (I'm not advocating these kinds of severe punishments, please understand. I'm saying I understand why a society would impose these kinds of severe punishments.)

Now, I know some people are NOT going to like this coldly logical conclusion, that emotion drugs really, truly are intrinsically bad things, because they use emotion drugs themselves on a regular basis, and they are going to whine about this and refuse to be convinced. Because they LIKE emotion drugs and don't want to give them up. So they'll DELIBERATELY stay dumb. They'd rather have dope than brains, man. They'll squinch their eyes shut as tight as they can, put their hands over their ears and refuse to believe a single word they've read. Emotion drugs are their refuge from reality, their escape from pain.

So I'm going to hit this one more time, harder. Let's look at this one more time, in more detail. Let's theoretically make emotion drugs legal, and see what happens to society, okay? Emotion drugs are legal, and corporations start fighting each other to sell them. What happens first? Emotion drugs get CHEAP. Cocaine, fifty cents a pound. Crack, one dollar a pound. Marijuana, two dollars for twenty one-ounce cigarettes. Heroin, five bucks a pound.

Sure, millions of people will get addicted and eventually kill themselves. You'll be stepping over dead bodies in the streets every day. Every city will have to have a crew that does nothing but pick up dead bodies. But we knew that's what was going to happen when we made emotion drugs legal. Hell, it's just cleaning up the gene pool. Just evolution in action, right?

And, yeah, intellectual, moral, and scientific progress will slow way the hell down because society will be collectively choosing NOT to get smarter. The smart people, instead of doing all the stuff smart people do, like inventing cures for cancer and AIDs and things like that, will be drooling against their bedroom wall stoned out of their friggin' minds.

What will happen along with this? Well, if people can use emotion drugs to get happy they will tend NOT to use any other method. So sales of high-speed race cars will go down, along with parachutes and airplanes and video games and whatever else you can name, because the only goal people really have, the ONLY reason they do whatever it is they do, every single action, no matter how small, is to get happy, as so fundamental a document as the Declaration of Independence recognizes.

When we made emotion drugs legal we made that the CHEAPEST way to get happy. So the VISIBLE start of the decline of society will be an economic crash, which will take a good while before it starts. The INVISIBLE part will be the intellectual decline. This will start immediately and actually have MUCH more severe effects, but you will NEVER see it happening. The only companies making money will be the emotion-drug companies.

What happens next? The emotion drugs get BETTER. Free-market competition, right? The first primitive generation of emotion drugs have an unfortunate tendency to damage and kill their users. This is like, you know, REAL bad from a profit standpoint. So the emotion-drug companies will engage in a research race to produce the best possible emotion drug, one that doesn't kill or damage their customers.

It is QUITE clear what the end of that research race will be. Say hello to the Happiness Box. The Happiness Box is the ultimate expression of the wire-to-the-brain thing, the ultimate emotion drug. It is a steel box designed to keep a human brain alive and happy, VERY happy. The way it's used is a living brain is removed from its body and placed in the box. Various wires and tubes are connected to the brain and the box is closed. Somebody punches the start button, and that brain goes into Nirvana and STAYS there, forever, or for as long as the brain or the box lasts, anyway. With the appropriate technology, this could easily be hundreds of years, maybe even thousands.

Various ruffles and flourishes are possible. For example, the most advanced version of the Happiness Box could, instead of just keeping you stoned all the time, be programmed so that you lived an artificial life inside the box. Of course, after the knowledge you were in a Happiness Box was removed, it would seem completely real to you.

Hmmph. It hits me the first primitive generation of Happiness Boxes are on the market RIGHT THIS SECOND, video games. Right? The user gets into what's already being described as a, "total immersive experience," and stays there in his own little world for hours and hours, completely isolated from the rest of reality. It's not unknown for people to play these things for days on end, without even sleeping. And to get addicted to them, too.

Yeah, Happiness Boxes are already headed our way, the Playstation 10,000, the ultimate XBox, SIMS become real, Azeroth forever and ever. Just drop your brain into it, close the lid, and press the Start button. These things will sell like hot cakes, won't they, folks? Perfect happiness living your perfect life forever, and no side-effects! People will be jumping into Happiness Boxes by the millions.

And there will be a TREMENDOUS push for everybody to jump into his own personal Happiness Box. Because as more and more people disappear, society is going to go downhill FAST. It will be a race to the bottom like nothing ever seen in history. And once the last person goes into the last Happiness Box, that will be the end of society. Society made emotion drugs legal, and the end result was the absolutely unavoidable, total destruction of society—and the Suicide of Man. Once again, oopsie.

Guess what we just found. We just found the mechanism by which sentient races go extinct. They reach the technological point where they can build Happiness Boxes, build them, jump into them, and disappear. When the last brain dies, as it must inevitably do, that race is extinct. Not with a bang, but with a whimper. Poof.

In the meantime, I note that in the real world, while emotion drugs are illegal, HAPPINESS BOXES ARE NOT. The world's societies haven't looked very far down the road when it comes to emotion drugs. Which makes sense, since they can't even define what an emotion drug is. So get ready, all you young people out there. The opportunity to buy your own Happiness Box and disappear into it is going to come within your lifetime. It's going to be entirely legal to do so.

Step right up and get'em while they're hot, folks. One hell of a debate is coming to this world. SHOULD I, OR SHOULD I NOT, JUMP INTO A HAPPINESS BOX? On the face of it, this seems a laughably absurd question. Of course, you should jump into a Happiness Box! Perfect happiness! Living a long time, maybe a thousand years! More! It's the SMART thing to do!

Sure, when the world's societies see what Happiness Boxes are doing to the world, they will try to make these Happiness Box thingies illegal, in order to stay in existence. But does a society really have that right? To punish people for using emotion drugs, Happiness Boxes, even when it's a certain thing that society, the human race itself, will be destroyed in the end? Does a society have the right to put its existence above the right of its members to get happy anyway they want to? Does the human race have a right to put its existence above the rights of its members to get happy anyway they want to?

The answer to this question doesn't matter. If enough people want it, and they will, Happiness Boxes WILL become legal. No matter what the answer is, no matter what it does to society, to the human race. The history of Prohibition teaches us that.

The world's societies are going to LOSE this War on Drugs, aren't they, folks? They don't have a snowball's chance in Hell, despite all the hundreds of billions they've spent. Society is going down, HARD. The clock is ticking, the fuse is lit, and it's only a matter of time until the explosion. Happiness Boxes are going to come out, and it's going to be Game Over for the human race in less than fifty years.

And why does that even matter? Where in Nature does it say

91

that human society HAS to exist? That the human race itself HAS to exist? Don't all species go extinct in the end anyway? It all seems just so inevitable and unavoidable. So why not just let it happen? In fact, why not start funding research into creating Happiness Boxes for everybody in the world immediately? Last one in is a rotten egg!

I mean, look at the real world. A world filled with horror, with death and dying, cancer and AIDS, with terrorists and suicide bombers and a million different painful ways of getting killed. A world---FILLED WITH UNHAPPINESS. Compared to perfect bliss and perfect safety inside a Happiness Box, is there anything in the world that could possibly offset that? That would make jumping into a Happiness Box a STUPID thing for an individual to do? Because that's the one thing that would stop this from happening. If there were some EXTREMELY powerful reason for an individual NOT to jump into a Happiness Box.

Is there such a reason? W-e-l-l, yes, there is, actually. There is ONE teeny little thing that could actually make it incredibly stupid for an individual to jump into a Happiness Box. So much so that he would look at this thing and then just walk away without so much as a backward glance at a lost Nirvana. But I have got to warn you all first. It is a truly BIZARRE reason. Lean back and take a breath. Brace yourselves.

The reason is: IF PEOPLE HAVE SOULS. If people have souls. That one thing, AND THAT ONE THING ONLY, would make it stupid to jump into a Happiness Box.

Allow me to explain. First, I must define precisely what I mean by "soul." A "soul" is an eternally existing thinking and feeling structure that survives the death of the physical body. Souls can and do inhabit physical bodies, but don't require one. In the simplest terms, a "soul" is you without a body, exactly the same except without a body.

So how would having a soul make it stupid to jump into a Happiness Box? Let's think about what would happen to you when you jumped into a Happiness Box and closed the lid, okay? Centuries and centuries and CENTURIES of unending pleasure and bliss. Then your brain dies, as it must do in the end. And your soul pops loose. It is thrown back into harsh, cold reality from the artificial Nirvana it's been in.

What kind of psychological condition is your soul in? How well is it going to get along with all the other souls out there? How strong is your soul going to be after centuries of bliss? About as strong as wet cardboard, huh, folks? Whatever lessons your soul learned about getting along with reality and all the other souls out there will have been wiped away by centuries of unending pleasure, haven't they? Just smoothed away and gone.

So all those painful lessons are going to have to be relearned all over again, painfully. And the pain won't just be yours, but for everybody else who has to deal with you, too. The danger is greater than it might appear. For somebody who has been in the simplest kind of Happiness Box, one where his bliss centers were stimulated, the end result will be the creation of a child, an infant. This will be an unpleasant thing to deal with, but not too unpleasant.

But worse is possible, MUCH worse. Consider somebody who has been in the most advanced type of Happiness Box, one where he has lived in an artificial reality designed to cater to his every whim. Centuries and centuries and CENTURIES of having his every desire fulfilled, of ALWAYS getting his own way. What kind of psychological effect would that have on a soul? It would turn that soul into a stone-raving sociopath, wouldn't it, folks? It would create a true screaming psycho. Somebody who would never take anybody else's feelings into account, who would stop short at nothing to get what he wants, not even murder. This is a bad thing, to say the least. There's going to be a great deal of pain and agony involved for that soul to get right again, to relearn old lessons, for that soul and everybody else who has to deal with that soul.

So, in the end, when the pleasure that soul experienced unlearning those lessons is weighed against the pain that soul and everybody else experienced for that soul to relearn those lessons, the pain will be the greater amount, FAR greater. Which makes jumping into a Happiness Box a STUPID thing to do in the first place.

If you DON'T have a soul, jumping into a Happiness Box is SMART. If you DO have a soul, jumping into a Happiness Box is STUPID. Note that which one is the smart thing to do is entirely dependent on whether or not you have a soul AND NOTHING ELSE.

So do you really, truly have a soul? That's the key thing you have to know when it becomes time to make that decision. It's far from an impossible thing, you know. There isn't any DEFINITIVE scientific evidence one way or the other. We can get an indication of the answer to this question by examining it from a somewhat abstract viewpoint. Let's look at this question from a societal viewpoint, by examining what the impact of immortal souls would be on a society.

How would everybody having immortal souls affect a society's behavior? You can examine this question by examining individual human behavior, too, and get the same answer, but we are talking about societies here, and so I restrict the argument here to societies.

What kinds of rules and regulations would an immortal-soul society have to have? One rule should be perfectly clear from all of the above. IN AN IMMORTAL-SOUL SOCIETY, YOU CAN'T GET HAPPY BY DIRECT STIMULATION OF YOUR EMOTION CENTERS. YOU CAN'T GET HAPPY BY ANY MEANS OTHER THAN

INTERACTING WITH OTHER SOULS AND THE UNIVERSE. In others words, emotion drugs HAVE to be ILLEGAL in an immortal-soul society, because, as we just saw, they create more pain than pleasure in the end. This is true of any kind of emotion drugs: no Happiness Boxes, no coke, no crack, and no heroin, and so on down the line. Although the line starts getting fuzzy eventually, because there will be certain substances, like marijuana and wine, that will have uses other than getting stoned. But it won't actually be necessary to pass laws making emotion drugs illegal. No SMART eternal being is going to touch these things. In a society of smart, self-aware eternal beings, a dope dealer will starve to death.

I gotta tell you, man, I see something quite incredibly strange here. You know that single, simple rule the world's stable societies are using regarding getting happy we abstracted up above? Compare it to the rule we just now derived about getting happy in an immortal-soul society. Do you see it? IT'S THE SAME DAMN RULE!

You can't get happy by using emotion drugs! Stable human societies are ALREADY acting like an immortal-soul society! Like we all have souls! When you try to find a good, solid reason why societies make emotion drugs illegal, the rock-bottom reason you eventually run into is the deep, deep assumption by all these stable societies that people really, truly are immortal souls!

Although nobody knows for a scientific fact souls exist, the world's stable societies ACT like they do. ALL of them. EVERY damn one! Funny thing, that. Y'all have a good one.

About the Author

Jeffrey A. Corkern is an analytical environmental chemist. Jeffrey A Corkern is a writer of science-based science fiction. Jeffrey A.

Corkern is the hardest of hard-case rationalists. Jeffrey A. Corkern is a professional cast-iron son of a *****

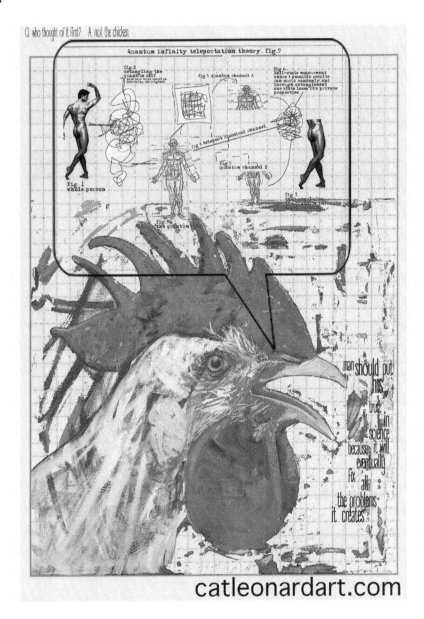

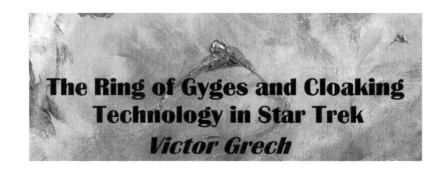

The Ring of Gyges and Cloaking Technology in Star Trek
Victor Grech

Introduction

No human has ever been invisible, a power that in legend is only attributed to gods and spirits. However, the possibilities inherent to the potential human acquisition of invisibility have been explored in several narratives. Plato (427-347 BC) reviewed this in the story of the Ring of Gyges. The myth recounts that Gyges was a shepherd in the service of King Candaules of Lydia. An earthquake exposed a cave mouth which Gyges stumbled upon. He discovered a tomb which contained a giant who wore a golden ring. This gave Gyges invisibility and he used this power to seduce King Candaules' queen. She then aided him in regicide, whereupon he became king of Lydia.

Satanically induced invisibility naturally also leads to wrong-doing. Christopher Marlowe's Mephastophilis and Faustus become invisible, visit the Vatican, shout insults at the pope, box his ears, beat friars, throw fireworks among them and exit laughing. More recently, Herbert George Wells in his *The Invisible Man* described a scientist who studied optics and invented a way to change his own refractive index to that of ambient air, thereby becoming invisible. He unfortunately failed to reverse the process, was betrayed by an acquaintance, and embarked on a reign of terror.

Even more recently, J. R. R. Tolkien's *The Hobbit* depicted a person who, like Gyges, discovers a ring that confers invisibility. The three sequels (*The Fellowship of the Ring*, *The Two Towers* and *The Return of the King*) showed that the Ring progressively corrupted its bearer, regardless of the purity of the bearer's original initial intentions. And most recently, an invisibility cloak is also seen in the *Harry Potter* series (Rowling).

In these narratives, it is almost as if the attainment of invisibility, a superhuman power, is a faustian hubristic desire that deserves the punishment of the gods, resulting in tragedy. This essay will explore invisibility in the Star Trek canon and will show that overall, the same tropes and outcomes are portrayed.

Narratives

The first time that cloaking technology is mentioned in the franchise is when a Romulan warship encounters the *Enterprise*. The ship's captain orders: "We grow visible. Attend the cloaking system" (McEveety, "Balance of Terror"). Earlier in the timeline, the Xyrillian race also use a cloaking device for their ship, which is referred to as a "stealth device" (Vejar, "Unexpected"). The *Enterprise's* science officer notes that "invisibility is theoretically possible, Captain, with selective bending of light. But the power cost is enormous" (McEveety, "Balance of Terror"), thereby conferring advantages to its users, and also disadvantages.

The early cloaking devices developed in the 22nd century did not completely cloak ships as these could still be detected as "a blip on the motion sensor" (McEveety, "Balance of Terror") or through the detection of "gas [...]. Under impulse power she expends fuel like any other vessel. We call it 'plasma' [...] it is merely ionised gas" (Meyer, *Star Trek VI: The Undiscovered Country*). Earlier in the *Star Trek* universe's timeline, Suliban ships are detected using information that is imparted to the *Enterprise* crew from the 31st century, well in their future. They are shown how to construct "quantum beacons [...] positron-based and have an output of two hundred gigawatts"

This technology is almost incomprehensible to the ship's chief engineer who has to "isolate the sub-assembly tolerances from the emitter algorithms" since the "assembly's independent of the emitters" and he must also "generate a stable flux between the positron conductors. Then all you'll have to do is renormalize the tertiary wave functions" (Kroeker, "Shockwave"). The engineer is equally baffled by the cloaking technology itself, and when a Suliban ship falls into his hands, he experiences significant difficulties in activating its cloak in order to attempt to rescue captured crewpersons. "We've still got that Suliban cell-ship, [...] I've been working on it in my free time. I'm pretty close to figuring out how it works. If I can bring the cloak on line, we can get past their defences, grab our people, and no one will see a thing." Tinkering with the system is initially fruitless. "I don't get it. The power converter is engaged. Juice is definitely flowing through these relays. So why can we still see the ship?" When he succeeds, a power overflow of some kind makes his right arm disappear for several hours. The doctor fails to sort out this problem since "quantum physics is hardly my speciality, but I'd guess that you received an intense dose of whatever particle radiation that ship uses to conceal itself. [...] I suspect your appendage will eventually re-materialise on its own," which proves to be the case (Contner, "The Communicator").

However, even this early in the timeline, Romulan ships were undetectable with "quantum beacons" (Contner, "Minefield"). A crude expedient allowing the exposure of cloaked ships is shown in the 24th century using a group of ships as a form of blockade. "Each ship will send out an active tachyon beam to the other blockading ships [...], any cloaked vessel that attempts to pass between our ships must cross that beam and be detected" (Carson, "Redemption Part 2").

In the Delta Quadrant, the alien species known as "the Swarm" used a similar technique to monitor the borders of their own territory, consisting of a series of interlaced tachyon beams. However, the *Voyager* crew devised a way to elude this grid by modifying their shields to refract the beams around the ship in an uninterrupted manner. "Their sensor net uses a series of interlaced tachyon beams. If we adjust our shields to refract those beams around the ship we can slip across without appearing to have disrupted the net" (Singer, "The Swarm").

But later in the 24th century, cloaking technology had been perfected. "No way of penetrating his cloak [...] he could pass within ten metres of every ship in Starfleet and they'd never know" (Baird, "Nemesis").

Cloaking Technology on the Large Scale

Several races are shown to have developed cloaking technology that encompasses entire vessels. These include the Romulans, Klingons, Suliban and Xyrillians. Species that run cloaked ships are often depicted as shifty and treacherous and this particularly applies to Romulans, whose very "heart itself is grey" (Livingston, "Inter Arma Enim Silent Leges"). Indeed, "Earth believes the Romulans to be warlike, cruel, treacherous" (McEveety, "Balance of Terror").

The technology itself has also been shown to cause problems even to species that are accustomed to using it. For example, the *Enterprise* crew discover an invisible ship trailing them in close proximity, "a hitchhiker [...] using some sort of stealth technology

100

[…] long enough to throw half our systems out of whack […] disrupting a number of […] systems." The alien Xyrillians apologise and explain that their "engines are malfunctioning" and they therefore used Enterprise's "plasma exhaust" and shared its warp field. When their systems malfunction again and they try the same tactic on a Klingon battleship, the same temporary havoc is wreaked with "unusual malfunctions […] problems with […] gravity plating, propulsion, environmental controls." The wrathful Klingons almost destroy the Xyrillian ship and it is only with the *Enterprise's* intercession that they eventually stand down (Vejar, "Unexpected"). Similarly, several cloaked ships are suspected to be trailing the Enterprise when the crew's sensors show "strange readings" and, "trouble balancing the warp field […]. It'll be stable one moment, and then, for no reason, it'll go slightly out of alignment. […]. We've had to realign the field a dozen times over the last hour" (Kroeker, "Shockwave").

> The largest cloaked object in the canon is an entire planet, Aldea, the wondrous mythical world […]. Advanced culture, centuries old. Self-contained, peaceful. Incredible technical sophistication providing the daily needs for all the citizens, so that they could turn themselves over to art and culture […]. Somehow, as the legend goes, the Aldeans were able to cloak their planet in darkness and go unseen by marauders, and other hostile passers-by who might rob and plunder.

This awesome feat is facile, theoretically speaking! "The theory is simple. The shield bends light rays around the planet's contour, similar to the Romulan cloaking device. But the implementation is quite difficult." It turns out however that the Aldeans

> need help from the Federation to rebuild […] heritage.
> We need a younger generation, strong and healthy,

following in the Aldean traditions [...]. Because we have no children, [...] medical community can do nothing [...]. We propose a trade. One which will solve our problem and give something back to the Federation [...]. We need some of your children. In payment, we will give you information that would take you centuries to acquire.

The *Enterprise* crew naturally refuses

That might be acceptable to some other races, but humans are unusually attached to their offspring [...]. Our children are not for sale at any price [...]. We sympathise with your situation, but what you ask is not possible [...]. That's my only answer. Now if there's some other way we can help you...

The Aldean spokesman regretfully states: "I am sorry you are intransigent" and the children are taken by force. "Captain, your children are with us. My word of honour, no harm will ever come to them [...]. Let us begin discussions regarding appropriate compensation."

Picard is rightfully incensed, "Compensation? You have stolen our children away from their classrooms, away from their bedrooms and you talk about compensation? You claim to be a civilised world and yet you have just committed an act of utter barbarity!" Fortunately, the *Enterprise* crew discover the cause of the Aldean infertility.

The radiation levels on Aldea have been building up over a long period of time. It is similar to what was experienced on Earth in the twenty-first century. When the ozone layer had deteriorated and the surface of the planet was flooded with ultraviolet radiation [...]. The shield that protected your world in one way is weakening it in another. It is the radiation of your own sun that is destroying you [...]. You're all suffering from radiation poisoning. Sterility is only the latest symptom. If the children remain, they will be affected as well.

The Aldeans therefore realise that "the very thing which has given us this wonderful world is what has caused this tragedy," and deactivate Aldea's cloak (Manners, "When The Bough Breaks").

Cloaking Technology on the Small Scale

A personal cloak is very similar to the examples given in the introduction of this essay, that is, to the rings of Gyges and Mordor, and to Wells' inventor's technological breakthrough. In *Star Trek*, cloaks are used by individuals to spy on the *Voyager* crew (Livingston, "Distant Origin"), to perform medical experiments on this same crew (Livingston, "Scientific Method") and to create surprise attacks in personal, hand-to-hand combat (Brooks, "The Abandoned"). The latter was shown to be a genetically created ability, known as a shroud, in an artificially engineered race of warriors, the Jem'Hadar. Yet another type of genetically engineered stealthing is shown in the Suliban cabal species who manage to evade detection through chameleon-like skin pigmentation changes (Conway, "Broken Bow"). The latter are also depicted as being evil and shifty, scurrying on all fours along walls and roofs. Mines are also cloakable, making them particularly devastating weapons. Early in the timeline, these are detectable using the abovementioned "quantum beacons" (Contner, "Minefield").

Discussion

Many researchers have acknowledged that

> [i]nvisibility has been a source of fascination and an
> inspiration of myths, novels and films, from the
> mythical magical artifact Ring of Gyges mentioned by
> the philosopher Plato in The Republic to the Cheshire
> Cat from Alice's Adventures in Wonderland and the
> ships in the Star Trek universe equipped with
> hardware known as cloaking devices that conceal them
> from most varieties of scans (Brun 1).

The story of the Ring of Gyges was narrated by Glaucon, a
student of Socrates, who then asked:

> Suppose now that there were two such magic rings, and
> the just [person] put on one of them and the unjust
> [person] the other; no man can be imagined to be of
> such an iron nature that he would stand fast in justice.
> No man would keep his hands off what was not his own
> when he could safely take what he liked out of the
> market, or go into houses and lie with any one at his
> pleasure, or kill or release from prison whom he would,
> and in all respects be like a god among men. Then the
> actions of the just would be as the actions of the unjust;
> they would both come at last to the same point. And
> this we may truly affirm to be of a great proof that a
> man is just, not willingly or because he thinks that
> justice is any good to him individually, but of necessity,
> for wherever any one thinks that he can safely be
> unjust, there he is unjust (Plato lines 360b-d).

In brief, Glaucon elaborates Baron John Emerich Edward Dalberg
Acton's more succinct maxim, "power tends to corrupt, and
absolute power corrupts absolutely" (Rawson 611).

Cloaking therefore encourages the manifestation of the Jungian shadow, since the "the seed of violence remains within each of us" (Wiemer, "Violations"). In the canon, the United Federation of Planets and Starfleet are depicted as the enlightened exemplars that humanity could and should aspire to emulate in a utopian future. It is as if for this very reason that humanity is denied cloaking technology, despite having stolen a device during an audacious raid on a Romulan vessel (Lucas, "The Enterprise Incident"). In Gene Roddenberry's own words, "our people are scientists and explorers – they don't go sneaking around" (Okuda 80).

It is later shown that the "Treaty of Algeron" (a peace accord between the Federation and the Romulan Empire) included the prohibition of the development or use of cloaking technology by the Federation (Burton, "The Pegasus"). This agreement is rarely infringed or circumvented. When the Federation is *in extremis*, with its very existence threatened by a powerful enemy ("The Dominion"), a specifically designed starship is shown to be able to cloak through the use of a Romulan-donated cloaking device (Friedman, "The Search"), with the stipulation that its cloak is only activated in Dominion territory, a clause which is occasionally broken with impunity (Conway, "The Way of the Warrior"). However, the ship's cloaking device does cause problems, and on one occasion, a transporter accident due to particle residue buildup from cloak use sends the transporting crewmembers back in time (Badiyi, "Past Tense, Part I")

Moreover, during the Dominion war, the Federation liberally used space mines that are cloaked (Kroeker, "Call to Arms"), and this does not result in any ill-effects to the Federation. Thus, *inter arma enim silent leges*, a Latin maxim attributed to Cicero that is commonly translated as "in times of war, the law falls silent." This is acknowledged within the canon, to the extent that it also constitutes the name of an episode (Livingston, "Inter Arma Enim

Silent Leges").

However, when Starfleet covertly creates a cloaking device and tests it on the starship *Pegasus*, an explosion in main engineering results in heavy casualties. Several members of the crew, including senior officers, mutinied during an attempt to shut down the test device. Despite the escaping crew witnessing an explosion, the ship drifted through an asteroid in a semi-dematerialised state and then rematerialized inside the asteroid. Despite efforts by Starfleet intelligence to hush up these events, the *Enterprise* crew discover the *Pegasus* and the surviving perpetrators are court-martialed (Burton, "The Pegasus").

Entire ships with cloaking technology have also been stolen by Starfleet officers, but are eventually returned to their owners (Nimoy, *Star Trek III: The Search for Spock*). At this juncture, it must be pointed out that as a corollary to Arthur C. Clarke's third law which states that "'any sufficiently advanced technology is indistinguishable from magic,' 'any sufficiently advanced technology is indistinguishable from a completely ad-hoc plot device'" (Langford). In other words, cloaking technology as evidenced in *Star Trek* is, as yet, unrealisable.

The only comparable technology is that of stealth, which is currently standard on virtually all new military aircraft by a combination of dark and radar-absorbing paint, optical camouflage, cooling the outer surface of the aircraft in order to minimize electromagnetic emissions, particularly infrared (heat) and the minimisation of all other electromagnetic and particulate emissions. Jamming technology for remote sensing devices is also utilised.

However, there may be science-fictional properties in metamaterials, artificial materials designed to have properties that are not normally found in nature. These may provide the theoretical possibility of allowing electromagnetic radiation to appear to pass freely through a cloaked object by going seamlessly around it, and are currently being studied (Service), and deemed theoretically possible (Petit).

In conclusion, if and when cloaking technology becomes available, "we must recognise that, because [...] violence is capable of consuming each of us" (Wiemer, "Violations"), this knowledge must be handled carefully lest we abuse it, as many other scientific discoveries have been abused.

Bibliography

Episodes and films

"Balance of Terror." Dir. Vincent McEveety. *Star Trek: The Original Series*. Paramount. December 1966.

"Broken Bow." Dir. James Conway. *Star Trek: Enterprise*. Paramount. September 2001.

"Call to Arms." Dir. Allan Kroeker. *Star Trek: Deep Space Nine*. Paramount. June 1997.

"Distant Origin." Dir. David Livingston. *Star Trek: Voyager*. Paramount. April 1997.

"Inter Arma Enim Silent Leges." Dir. David Livingston. *Star Trek: Deep Space Nine.* Paramount. March 1999.

"Minefield." Dir. James A. Contner. *Star Trek: Enterprise*. Paramount. October 2002.

"Past Tense, Part I." Dir. Reza Badiyi. *Star Trek: Deep Space Nine*. Paramount. January 1995.

"Redemption II." Dir. David Carson. *Star Trek: The Next Generation*. Paramount. September 1991.

"Scientific Method." Dir. David Livingston. *Star Trek: Voyager*. Paramount. October 1997.

"Shockwave, Part I." Dir. Allan Kroeker. *Star Trek: Enterprise*. Paramount. May 2002.

"The Abandoned." Dir. Avery Brooks. *Star Trek: Deep Space Nine*. Paramount. October 1994.

"The Communicator." Dir. James A. Contner. *Star Trek: Enterprise*. Paramount. November 2002.

"The Enterprise Incident." Dir. John Meredyth Lucas. *Star Trek: The Original Serie*s. Paramount. September 1968.

"The Pegasus." Dir. LeVar Burton. *Star Trek: The Next Generation.* Paramount. January 1994.

"The Search, Part I." Dir. Kim Friedman. *Star Trek: Deep Space Nine*. Paramount. September 1994.

"The Swarm." Dir. Alexander Singer. *Star Trek: Voyager*. Paramount. September 1996.

"The Way of the Warrior." Dir. James L. Conway. *Star Trek: Deep Space Nine*. Paramount. October 1995.

"Unexpected." Dir. Mike Vejar. *Star Trek: Enterprise*. Paramount. October 2001.

"Violations." Dir. Robert Wiemer. *Star Trek: The Next Generation*. Paramount. February 1992.

"When the Bough Breaks." Dir. Kim Manners. *Star Trek: The Next Generation*. Paramount. February 1988.

Star Trek III: The Search for Spock. Dir. Leonard Nimoy. Paramount. 1984.

Star Trek VI: The Undiscovered Country. Dir. Nicholas Meyer. Paramount 1991.

Star Trek: Nemesis. Dir. Stuart Baird. Paramount. 2002.

Secondary texts

Brun Michele, Sebastien Guenneau and Alexander B. Movchan. "Achieving control of in-plane elastic waves." *Applied Physics Letters* 94.6 (2008): 061903

Marlowe Christopher. *The Tragical History of the Life and Death of Doctor Faustus.* London: Valentine Simmes, 1604.

Clarke Arthur C. *Profiles Of The Future.* London: Pan Books, 1973.

Langford David. "A Gadget Too Far." *New Worlds 2.* Ed. David Garnett.

New York: Gollancz, 1992.

Okuda Michael, Denise Okuda and Debbie Mirek. *The Star Trek Encyclopedia a Reference Guide to the Future Updated and Expanded Edition.* New York: Pocket Books, 1997.

Petit Charles. "Invisibility uncloaked: In race to make things disappear, scientists gain ground on science fiction." *Science News* 176 (2009): 18–23.

Plato. *The Republic.* New York: Vintage, 1991.

Rawson Hugh and Margaret Miner. *The Oxford Dictionary of American Quotations.* New York: Oxford UP, 2006

Rowling J. K.. *Harry Potter and the Philosopher's Stone.* London: Bloomsbury Publishing, 1997.

Service Robert F and Adrian Cho. "Strange New Tricks With Light". *Science* 330 (2010): 1622.

Tolkien J. R. R. *The Fellowship of the Ring.* London: George Allen & Unwin, 1954.

Tolkien J. R. R. *The Hobbit*. London: George Allen & Unwin, 1937.

Tolkien J. R. R. *The Return of the King*. London: George Allen & Unwin, 1955.

Tolkien J. R. R. *The Two Towers*. London: George Allen & Unwin, 1954.

Wells Herbert George. *The Invisible Man. A Grotesque Romance*. London: C. Arthur Pearson, 1897.

About the Author

Victor Grech was a science fiction (SF) fan from a young age. Although he studied medicine and became a pediatrician, he remains a physicist at heart, with an enduring interest in astronomy, astrophysics and cosmology. The allure of SF eventually led to his reading for a Ph.D. in the University of Malta's English Language Department entitled "Infertility in Science Fiction." The thesis was completed in 2011. Several scholarly publications have arisen from this work, as well as other publications that deal with various aspects of SF. The thesis classified infertility in SF according to theme, for example, after warfare, terrorism, state inflicted, alien inflicted, affecting aliens or animals etc. Over three hundred primary texts were considered and the one commonality that ensued was SF's inherent optimism. SF is the modern replacement of the fairy tale, and therefore, almost invariably terminates in a happy ending, just like a fairy tale. Instead of monsters, we have aliens. Instead of magic, one finds advanced technologies. The end result is the same, the willing suspension of disbelief and an abiding sense of wonder. Subsequent papers have mostly focused on Star Trek, since this provides an enormous corpus of material for potential study. He continues to read SF in his spare time and greatly enjoys watching SF films and series (such as Star Trek) with his two children who have also become enamored of the genre.

2016 marks the 50th anniversary from the launch of Star Trek: The Original Series. To commemorate such an event, the organisers are planning the second Star Trek Symposium.

This will differ from the traditional Fan-Based Convention in that it will be a platform for academics from across many disciplines to meet and explore this particular intersection between the Humanities and the Sciences.

The first Star Trek Symposium held in 2014 was well received, thus motivating the organizers to celebrate Star Trek's Golden Anniversary with this second event.

The Symposium will be held under the auspices of HUMS, the Humanities, Medicine and Sciences Programme at the University of Malta. The Star Trek Symposium will appeal to both scientists and fans of science fiction. Come and join us in Malta!

Web: www.startreksymposium.com
Email: info@startreksymposium.com

Why we are here?

Roy Gray

Yes that is the title, it's not a typo for 'why are we here?' It is meant to suggest that what follows may answer some philosophical questions and mysteries. In these surroundings you may think this is fiction, and perhaps it is, but the line of reasoning hangs together so well and explains so much that such a conclusion would really disappoint.

The mysteries referred to include: the Fermi paradox; the outcome of WWII; our avoidance of nuclear conflagration; the rise of science and democracy. Additionally it may bear on how catastrophic climate change and other potentially destructive events might be avoided.

Scientists use creative language to describe their activities. Statements like 'probing the microwave background to see the universe when it was only 350,000 years old' or 'looking back to the big bang'. In effect, they are receiving information now from the universe in its infancy. No one is looking back in time, but they are examining objects now using the radiation (light) emitted in the distant past. To reiterate: the astronomers and cosmologists made their observations recently, all obvious but all-important.

The English language is uncomfortable with concepts such as 'being outside time' so here terms like 'before' and 'after' will not always have their normal meaning. In such cases, these words will be in single quotation marks.

Scientists have used the anthropic principle as an explanation for the structure of the universe. Simply put, this means the cosmos must be like it is because humans are here. Cosmologists then worry because this means certain fundamental constants have to be very precise and they can't explain that without resorting to a plethora of multi-dimensional string theory universes with humans happening to exist in the one that supports life as we know it. So the question of why remains unanswered.

The anthropic principle is perhaps a clue, but not the complete answer.

Stephen Hawking and Thomas Hertog have devised a theory of the universe based on its emergence from a state where quantum effects ruled. They termed this the 'Flexiverse'. Present theories of quantum gravity are moot, so the early universe remains a mystery but there are clues, and observations are closing in on the event. For instance NASA's WMAP satellite observations of polarisation in the microwave background are said to have provided clues to the state of the universe at an extremely short interval, 10^{-35} seconds, 'after' the Big Bang. The word 'after' is used advisedly as Hawking and Hertog said that the quantum mechanics-ruled 'region' of the universe had no time dimension but four spatial dimensions.

Without going into detail, Hawking and Hertog have called their ideas the 'no-boundary proposal'. They describe a Flexiverse with no singularity, no definable origin point and, from our timebound viewpoint, a universe expanding from a tiny region ruled by quantum mechanics. A godlike observer outside all of this, and so 'outside time' might 'see' a huge balloon of possibilities. A close inspection would 'show' this 'balloon' as being made up of innumerable intertwined threadlike tracks, each with its own miniscule quantum region at one point or more; and, in many cases, a giant, classical stars and galaxies cosmos elsewhere. The totality of all those threads is that Flexiverse, the balloon from the outsider viewpoint. Each track within the Flexiverse is an alternative/potential universe.

One of these has humanity and the Earth at one point and Hawking's quantum region at another. There are 13.7 billion years between those points according to astronomers on Earth now. Each 'track' or 'path' is called a "history" and according to Hawking our present universe is the "sum over histories" taking all paths into consideration.

That early quantum region can be said to be a version of Schrödinger's cat, a famous analogy scientists use to try to illuminate the mystery of the quantum world. Imagine a cat sealed in a box with a vial of poison gas and a single radioactive atom. If the atom decays, the radiation releases the poison and the cat dies; if not it lives. No one knows the cat's fate until they look inside the box. The decay is a quantum event; it could be said to happen at random, though scientists talk about probability. So until someone looks, is the cat dead or alive? Not knowing, the cat is said to be both dead and alive. Science calls that a superposition. Only when someone checks is it one or the other.

The nub of this argument lies in the possibility that, in some theories, the observer affects the quantum state. The cat's fate is sealed when someone looks in the box. But the light entering the observer's eye takes a finite time to arrive. The cat is dead, or not, before any observer gets the message because they cannot see it in the superposition. The cat's fate was decided by the act of observing before the light arrived, **effect and cause happen 'simultaneously'.**

Now apply that thinking to the entire universe. Its 'early' quantum state is not a simple binary, alive or dead choice, but much more complex. However every time scientists look into that quantum region they are doing the equivalent of opening, or looking into, the box. Let's say the quantum state of the universe

115

lasts 10^{-35} seconds. (That's as close as we've got so far.) The Planck time, the shortest possible time interval by present reckoning is 10^{-43} seconds. Of course Hawking says there is no time dimension at this 'time' but it is easier to think in terms of time rather than four-dimensional space with no time. Those numbers give us 10^8 (one hundred million) intervals to probe 'close' to the origin, 10^8 boxes to open, each one 13.7 billion years in the past but each observation, or measurement, producing a simultaneous effect.

This quantum region is vital, but so is the observer. No observer, equals no event, equals no human universe. The astronomers of today and the future are the observers. I am arguing that we are here because there is a causal link from the earliest stages of the universe to human astronomers making the measurements. From the godlike outsider viewpoint (outside time and space and the Flexiverse) the boxes have all been opened; from our human early 21st century viewpoint most of them are still closed. WMAP may yet open some but LISA, the proposed space-based gravitational wave detection system, will open even more. LISA will be a fleet of satellites linked by lasers that will detect the signals and send them back to Earth.

A ground-based system (LIGA) is also underway but this is unlikely to be sensitive enough to open any boxes, though it should detect merging black holes and close neutron stars.

Fermi asked where are all those alien space travellers, why aren't they here? The answer is that our astronomy is ahead of theirs and 'we are opening the boxes'. There may well be millions of sentient species in the universe but none have developed high-technology astronomy, and hence the capability to cross the galaxy, because humanity has shut them out.

Why did we avoid nuclear conflagration? Because that path would have prevented future astronomers from building the instruments we are using, and will use, to 'probe' the very earliest moments that define this universe.

WWII, the rise of science and democracy? Any other outcome would surely have restricted liberties and freethinking and prevented the advances in science that enables, and will enable, astronomers to make those observations.

Avoidance of future catastrophes? We have to link them to astronomy and physics, (e.g. build instruments and observatories in earthquake-prone regions or on worryingly quiescent volcanoes). Some catastrophes are already linked in the sense that if climate change could destroy the capability to make high-tech astronomical observations, then can it happen to that extent?

There is an argument that all humanity's eggs are in one basket and it should colonise space and other planets to avoid a disaster that would destroy civilisation, the planet or both. That move could precipitate the feared disaster because astronomy would carry on elsewhere. (Fermi again?)

Another worry would be the development of artificial intelligence (AI) capable of astronomy and cosmology, because then there may not be a 'need' for humans. Alternatively, AI might precipitate the much discussed technological singularity by opening the hundred million boxes rather quickly and bring our sum over history to an end; a scenario that seems to hold religious overtones and evoke Arthur C. Clarke's Nine Billion Names of God.

This proposal is not the anthropic principle. Hawking and Hertog have suggested:

- That the universe has a quantum mechanics-governed region that, from our viewpoint, defines its beginning.
- That the sum of histories encompassing the totality of possible universes linked to such a quantum region is the

117

universe humanity inhabits.

- "Top down" cosmology, based on what is observed in the universe now, should replace "bottom up" cosmology, based on working forward from a specified initial state for the universe.

Does the result of their thinking mean today's and tomorrows' astronomical observations affect those early universe quantum processes and, as humanity is the observer, that this is a direct link from here to then? If so, we risk interrupting it at our peril.

About the Author

Roy Gray's short stories, and even 'poetry', have appeared in magazines, (eg *Interzone*) anthologies, journals, trade press and online. He is not the Roy Gray who writes erotic poetry which also can be found online. Roy's chapbook 'The Joy of Technology', Pendragon Press 2011 and now a self-published ebook, could persuade some he is that other Roy Gray, but there are at least two of them, and this Roy's poetic efforts remain decidedly chaste. Roy won two Science in Print (Physics in Print) awards (back in the '90's) and, in collaboration with Phil Emery, a UK Public Awareness of Science grant in 2003. His non-fiction has appeared in *Physics World, Packaging India,* online and in *Interzone Magazine*. He has a degree in Physics and retired from a major pharmaceutical company in 2001. His speciality was packaging for new products. He lives in Macclesfield, a small town in North West England. More about Roy's E book 'The Joy of Technology' can be found at Roy's blog, see http://roy444.wordpress.com/

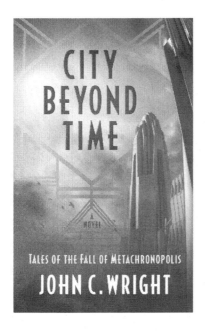
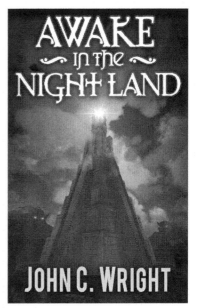

"John C. Wright is one of the greatest wordsmiths alive. The man is brilliant."
- Larry Correia, *New York Times* bestselling author

"Wright may be this fledgling century's most important new SF talent."
- *Publishers Weekly*

CASTALIA HOUSE
www.castaliahouse.com

The Philosophy of *Serenity*

Anthony Marchetta

Serenity is the movie sequel to Joss Whedon's famously short-lived sci-fi classic *Firefly*. Like the original series it got very good to excellent reviews, is adored by fans, bombed in theaters, and ended up making back the money anyway with spectacularly good DVD sales. Color me a fan. *Serenity* is a classic, one of the best sci-fi movies ever made with killer dialogue, terrific acting, and some genuinely intelligent plot twists that had me gasping appreciatively in impressed surprise.

To give a little bit of background, Serenity is the name of the spaceship that carries the movie's main cast. We start off with the Doctor, Simon; the first mate, Zoe; the pilot, Wash; the mercenary, Jayne; the mechanic, Kaylee; and the real stars of the movie, River, Simon's psychologically disturbed and psychic little sister; and Captain Malcolm "Mal" Reynolds. They're soon joined by Inara, a Companion (prostitute). They also have a couple of brief scenes with a Christian preacher named Shepherd Book. I mention him because he was a main character in the original *Firefly* series.

The plot starts off slowly, but this is more than compensated for by the killer dialogue. Every character gets a few one-line zingers in, and Whedon handles the ensemble cast beautifully. Simon and River Tam are fugitives on the run from the Alliance, this universe's version of the Evil Empire, and through events revealed in the original TV series they've fallen in with the crew of Serenity. Seventeen-year-old, ninety-pound River, played to perfection by

Summer Glau, is harboring a secret and the Alliance wants to make sure it doesn't get out. The unraveling of this secret, and what to do about it once it's revealed, makes up the main plot of the movie, though of course there's a lot more to it.

Joss Whedon is a famously virulent and ultra-feminist atheist. He is also, of course, an excellent writer, and, in my experience, good writers will tend to echo known truths about human nature even when they don't necessarily want to face it themselves. You can see a lot of this in atheist Douglas Adams. The Hitchhiker's Guide books are really about a man staring into the void and seeing nothing back. The only way to keep from crying in the face of such nothingness is to laugh. Adams recognized this, and it's this philosophical underpinning that makes the series so brilliant.

And so it is with Joss Whedon's *Serenity*. The real theme of the movie is man's underlying need for faith. Shepherd Book says it the most clearly when he tells Mal, "I don't care what you believe in, just believe in it" Of course, there's something deeper going on with that line that Whedon probably never intended. He is literally saying that it's better to believe in a lie than to look into the void and find nothing; it's better just to make up a substitute to fool yourself.

This isn't only an atheist idea. C.S. Lewis explores this concept in the climactic scene of the fourth Chronicles of Narnia book, *The Silver Chair*. The character of Puddlegum is talking to the Lady of the Green Kirtle. The children and he are being enchanted to believe that the real world is only make-believe and the dark underworld they're in is the only world that is:

"Suppose we have only dreamed, or made up, all those things— trees and grass and sun and moon and stars and Aslan himself. Suppose we have. Then all I can say is that, in that case, the made-up things seem a good deal more important than the real ones.

Suppose this black pit of a kingdom of yours is the only world. Well, it strikes me as a pretty poor one. And that's a funny thing, when you come to think of it. We're just babies making up a game, if you're right. But four babies playing a game can make a play-world which licks your real world hollow. That's why I'm going to stand by the play world. I'm on Aslan's side even if there isn't any Aslan to lead it. I'm going to live as like a Narnian as I can even if there isn't any Narnia. So, thanking you kindly for our supper, if these two gentlemen and the young lady are ready, we're leaving your court at once and setting out in the dark to spend our lives looking for Overland. Not that our lives will be very long, I should think; but that's a small loss if the world's as dull a place as you say."

This seems to us like a radical line of thought. It's practically blasphemous by modern standards. Lewis is literally saying that it's better to believe in a lie than believe in nothing at all. But does Whedon really say anything different? Shepherd Book is supposedly a Christian. This entails belief in things like the Resurrection of Christ and the importance of evangelization and repentance. Mal is supposedly an atheist. Book's number one priority, then, should be to convert Mal to Christianity. But that's not what he does! For Book, being a Christian is of secondary importance to Mal leaving behind the black hole of unbelief he has fallen into. Book doesn't care what Mal believes in. Like Lewis, Book recognizes that even believing in a lie is better than believing in nothing. Whedon, an excellent writer, senses this even if he doesn't state the idea outright. Atheism as a worldview is ultimately dead; the only way to survive it is to avoid its implications.

And so *Serenity* is really Mal's story about finding a meaning and a purpose to his life in the absence of a God to guide him. Some might say that this is a depressing idea. I found it a fascinating one. Ultimately, the driving force in Mal's life, the thing that gives him purpose and brings back his faith in humanity is bringing the truth to the world. Once again, Whedon can't help but stray towards a worldview that's probably more religious than he'd care to admit. If you're not going to be devoted to God, being devoted to uncovering the truth isn't such a bad next best thing. Book may have been on the right path after all—if you become devoted to finding the truth, you end up one step closer to God whether you intend to go there or not.

Nathan Fillion carries Mal's character arc brilliantly. We need to see a total transformation for Mal—not quite Scrooge level, but certainly a large emotional range. At one point Mal is in such a dark place that he's willing to abandon members of his crew on a dead planet, and by the end of the movie he's actually waxing poetic about love. This is not an easy arc to pull off, but Nathan Fillion is up to the task. His portrayal of Mal is one of the highlights of the movie.

Even more interesting is the evolution of Mal's character from the first "Serenity", the name of the show's pilot episode, and the movie's *Serenity*. At the end of the original one of the show's iconic lines became "We're still flying. That's enough." Mal doesn't care about anybody but himself and his crew; he's beyond the hope of saving the world. In contrast to this is the turning point of the movie "Serenity". When Mal decides he has a duty to reveal the truth to the world, he utters the now commonly quoted line "I aim to misbehave." Mal is no longer interested in just avoiding the Alliance; now he wants to actively cause them trouble.

The villain of the piece, the Operative, shows the problem with Whedon's philosophy of finding any cause you feel strongly about and making that your god. As the character of Inara says, what makes the Operative so dangerous is that he's a believer; he genuinely believes that when he commits mass genocide, he's doing the right thing. And if it doesn't matter what you believe in, what truly makes him so different from Mal in the end? Of course, the real point that Whedon was trying to make is that Mal never had a chance against the Operative until he found a cause he too was willing to stake his life on; only then was he a real match. Even here, we see shades of religious thinking. We're supposed to side with Mal because it's supposed to be essentially self-evident that what he's doing is right and what the Operative is doing is wrong. And it's true—it is. But given the philosophy we see presented, there's no way to really make sense of this without appealing to naturally evident, objective right and wrong—natural law, and part of Mal's rebirth is his rediscovery of the importance of objective good and objective evil.

Ultimately, *Serenity* is almost a parable about the importance of faith, man's search for meaning, and the simple self-evident boundaries present between right and wrong. It is a brilliant work and in my opinion it is, if not Whedon's finest hour (that might still go to the episode "Objects in Space", which deserves its own article), certainly better than "The Avengers", which had worse acting, a less interesting villain, and no real philosophical point of view to work from. Whedon does an excellent job of showing the importance of man's search for meaning—and in doing so, he lays bare the emptiness promised to those who truly embrace atheism. Stare into the void long enough, you become bitter, depressed, and angry—but if you find a cause to fight for, then maybe you'll realize that life might just be worth living after all.

Bibliography

Lewis, C.S. "The Silver Chair, Chapter Twelve." Red Library. 7 Sept. 1953. Web. 6 Jan. 2015.

Serenity. Universal Pictures, 2005. DVD.

About the Author

Anthony Marchetta is a twenty-year-old college student who started reading science fiction last summer and loved it. His short stories "A Quadrillion Occupied Planets" and "Take Up Your Cross" have been published in previous issues of the *Sci Phi Journal*. He is currently working on several short stories as well as a novel that makes good use of the Arthurian legends. He is, as always, very proud to be able to tell people that he's been published alongside the other fine authors of the Journal. He dedicates this story to his friend Matt O, who first introduced him to *Firefly*. Remember Matt, this whole thing is your fault. Anthony can be contacted at noblesquire1@aol.com

Novellete

HMS Mangled Treasure
The Rescue of Mr. Spaghetti by L. Jagi Lamplighter

"Pirates, you say?" asked the detective who stood on Clara's front step. At least Clara thought he was a detective, since he wore a fedora and a trench coat, and looked disturbingly like a Humphrey Bogart clone. He could have been the claims adjuster, however. She had talked to so many people, she had lost track.

Clara put her fists on her hips. "Listen here, Buster. Maybe you want me to lie to you—like that punk of an ex of mine did last time this happened. Tell you some comfortable story about car thieves and let it go at that. But that ain't gonna happen!" She shook her head for emphasis, sending her many cornrows flying and wagged a finger at him. "I'm one woman who respects the truth, and that. Is. Not. Going. To. Change!"

Usually, this was the place where they shot her the "you should be locked away" look. This guy just nodded calmly, like he was on the set of *Dragnet* or something. Cool as a cucumber, he was.

"Pirates towed your car, ma'am. Is that right?" he asked again. He spoke with a Bronx drawl, so that his "that" sounded like "dat". Clara had never heard a Bronx accent in real life. She kept expecting him to drop it and talk like a real human being.

"Yes!" she snapped.

"That's all right, ma'am. I believe you."

"You... you do?"

"Sure thing, ma'am. These pirates have been towing cars all over town."

Clara sighed. It felt good to have someone believe her for a change. It had been a while since anyone had believed her about anything. Still, it took all the fight out of her.

"Any idea who's behind it?" she asked as nicely as she was able.

The detective nodded solemnly. "A pack of the worst supernatural scum in Fairydom."

Just great. It would be that the guy who finally believed her was three crayons short of a box. Clara cocked her head and fixed him with the look that her miserable excuse of an ex used to call the Hairy Eye.

"Faeries towed my car?"

The detective met her gaze square on, completely unfazed by the Hairy Eye. That in itself was amazing.

"Ma'am," he drawled, "you just told me that pirates stole your car and sailed away—in the middle of Chicago, and I believed you. Common etiquette dictates you should extend to me the same courtesy."

Clara frowned. The guy seemed calm and reasonable. Not what she expected from a crazy, but then she had been an ER doc, not a psychiatrist. Maybe real crazies were as cool as cucumbers. It would certainly explain why he dressed and talked as if he had walked out of a 1940s movie.

"Look here, Mr. Spade-wanna-be. Pirates is one thing..." Clara froze, her mouth wide open, because at that moment, she remembered something.

A terrible sensation spread through her body, much like what she imagined it might feel like to be stung by scorpions. Tears pricked threateningly at her eyes. She let out a low warble of a moan.

"Mr. Spaghetti!" she wailed. "He's locked in the car!"

"Is that your dog, ma'am?" the detective asked.

Clara shook her head, nearly whipping him with her cornrows. Next time, she would stand a little closer and whap him good.

"No. A doll. My son's favorite doll." It shamed her that her voice broke. "He's going to be inconsolable."

"Children lose dolls all the time, ma'am. Part of life."

Clara turned on the poor man, showing her teeth like a wolf. "Is that so? Why don't you come home and explain it to my son. He's eight years old, weighs nearly seventy pounds, and has the language capacity of a delayed two-year-old. You come over to my house tonight, and you explain to Sammy what happened to his Mr. Spaghetti!"

The detective lowered the brim of his fedora. "I'll get your car back, ma'am."

#

Clara lay on her stomach among the trees at the Lincoln Park Zoo and peered through her binoculars. The ground was damp and cold under her shirt. She hoped this would not take too long. Behind her, she could hear the voices of laughing children as a school group toured the exhibits. This caused a pang of maternal longing, as she suddenly missed her own two kids.

131

According to her research into recent car thefts—she had called her sister's hunky friend at the police department—the roadside parking area she had under surveillance was a likely spot for the car thieves to hit and just after morning rush hour was a likely time. Pre-dawn would have been better, but she had been forced to wait until after Sari and Sammy had left for school.

Twelve cars had disappeared from this parking area alone in the last week. Like hers, they had all been parked off by themselves, with no one behind them. Of course, that did not mean one would disappear today, while she was watching, but she could hope.

And hope she did! It had taken a whole boatload of effort to rearrange her schedule so she could have today off. It would be weeks before she could arrange another free day. She had to horde her precious time off for when Sammy was home. It was hard enough to arrange things so that she did not have to work weekends.

To judge from last night's reaction, her household would not survive another day without Mr. Spaghetti, much less weeks!

Clara rubbed the bump on the bridge of her nose from where it had broken during the fit Sammy threw the last time Mr. Spaghetti went missing two years ago, the time they had accidentally left the rag-doll at the grocery store. She used to have a beautiful nose. People on the street would stop her and tell her how she could be a model. Of course, that was ten years and forty pounds ago. Today, she had more important things to worry about than whether her looks could make strangers gawk.

Besides, what had her looks ever gotten her except her good-for-nothing ex?

Clara lowered her head, resting it on her hands. How had her life come to this? Ten years ago, it had been filled with such promise!

She had grown up in the slums, no one in her family had ever finished high school. No one in her family had ever amounted to much of anything, until Clara came along.

Clara had finished high school. She had finished college. She had gone all the way through seven years of medical school! Clara had become a doctor! When her Mamma was young, women did not become doctors, much less women of color. Yet, Mamma's little girl had become one of the top physicians in the Mercy Hospital Emergency Room. She had saved lives!

She still had a vase of dried flowers on her mantelpiece, the remnants of the first bouquet given to her by someone whose life she saved.

She had given all this up for Sammy.

Clara recalled back to when Sammy was a baby. He had been the sweetest thing in the early months, even happier and less troublesome than his older sister, Sari. Even the Second Coming of Christ Himself could not have been sweeter!

But by two, he still was not talking, and he had started doing things with his hands, odd things that made him stand out from other children, holding them funny and waving them in front of his face. By five, he still was not talking, he still did weird things with his hands, and he was still throwing fits—the kind of fits her friends' children had stopped throwing at three or four. Then, her so-called-friends stopped bringing their children over to play with Sammy.

And the screaming! Bright lights set him off. Cleaning products in the air set him off. Dyes in the food set him off. And not being allowed to eat the brightly colored candies the other children ate. That set him off the worst of all.

At first, Stan went into denial. He tried to cover for Sammy, when the boy was young, to hide it. But by the time he had a six-year-old who was still in diapers and who bent over and gestured oddly while moaning in public, even Stan, Master of De Nile himself, could not hide it anymore. He started saying that Sammy was not his son, even accused Clara of having an affair!

Her, Clara, the ultimate good girl! Boy, she let him have it for that one!

Of course, it had not always been like that. Once, Stan had been the husband she was so proud of, so handsome and buff. She gave the tear on her cheek a vicious wipe. Did no good to focus on the past. Just made a girl feel sad. Had to stay focused on the present.

It had been her decision to leave the ER and stay home full time to take care of Sammy that had really ruined things. Stan did not like losing the status of his doctor wife, and he did not like losing her six digit paycheck, not one bit. He tried to have Sammy put in an institution. When Clara would not go along, he bugged out. Took his sorry ass and ran.

Well, good riddance to him! She didn't need a man like that anyhow.

Stan sent money, but it was never enough. He spent most of what he made on his new wife and their perfect little girl. Clara was reduced to working at Smarty-Mart.

Smarty-Mart! From a top Emergency Room physician to the manager at a Smarty-Mart. It was enough to make a lesser woman cry.

But Clara was not a lesser woman. She was a survivor. If sacrificing her hard-won career to become a manager at the Smarty-Mart was what God required in order to give her son a good life, that was what she was going to do!

It did not mean that she did not break down and bawl like a baby now and then—usually at night when no one was awake to see. But she sure as heck did not sit around grousing about what life had thrown her way, like some people she knew.

By and large, now that she thought about it, that was true of all the mothers of "Special Needs" children she knew. Being active on her son's behalf had led her to meet a lot of other mothers of children with problems "in the spectrum." They were a surprisingly resilient lot—not counting the one or two who could not hack it. There was a reason that their mutual support group was called Mothers From Hell!

These mamas were not going to let anyone keep their children from having the best life possible to them!

And it was all worth it, of course. Sammy might not be like other children. He might not talk clearly. He might flail his limbs when he got upset, sometimes even hurting his mother or sister. All that vanished, however, when she looked at him and saw his steady, shining eyes gazing back at her with such love, such trust.

It was like gazing directly at his soul, like looking into the eyes of an angel!

One smile from Sammy made all the crap worth it!

From somewhere above the tree tops came a very strange sound. Clara stiffened and listened. Voices, she thought, like a chorus. Only the voices were cold and eerie, and soulless, and filled with a harsh glee that had nothing to do with gladness.

> "The crew of the Mangled Treasure are we,
>
> Fearless and peerless and wicked and free!
>
> Deathless and pitiless robbers are we;
>
> Our hearts be as restless and cold as the sea!

We do not bleed blood and we cannot weep tears!

Our hearts are as empty and deep as our years!

Sing yo ho, me bullies, and heave with a will,

We sail over ocean and hamlet and hill;

Cold iron, man's iron, our plunder-holds fill,

For men are our cattle and we wish them ill!"

"This one will do, lads!" called out a single deep gravelly voice.

Clara's blood turned to ice in her veins. It was the middle of the morning! A God-fearing woman like her should be at work. What was she doing out hunting demented car thieves?

Her thoughts turned one last time to Sammy. To the look of hurt and desperation that had come over his dear face when his beloved Mr. Spaghetti had not been in his proper comforting place last night. She had to get that doll back!

Clara brought the binoculars up to her eyes and stared. Her jaw gaped. Even though she had caught a glimpse of these thieves twice before, it had not prepared her for what she saw now.

A huge square-rigger with sails the color of swamp fog mist sailed down out of the cloudy sky. The mainmast bore the symbol of a bleeding moon and a Jolly Roger flew from the foremast. Aboard the vessel was a crew of pirates, but not like the pirates in any book or movie!

Short, squat men in long jackets and boots with crimson sailor's hats served as powder monkeys. They toiled to and fro carrying rocks to the cannons. Huge, hulking creatures manned the guns, their tri-cornered hats, vests, and breeches were of bark and dead leaves. Tiny winged pixies, no bigger than Clara's finger, swarmed about the lookout. They were not cute, pretty creatures, like from a story book, but cruel, nasty little things with ugly, distorted faces. In their hands, they held shiny copper cutlasses.

At the helm stood a leering old man with a long, white beard. He was covered in barnacles and seaweed and wore a conch shell for a hat. To his left, a horrifyingly ugly creature with an enormous nose and no mouth at all. It leaned precariously over the railing, holding what appeared to be a pistol made of peat.

The captain and his officers were of another cut. Clara trained her binoculars upon them in fascination. These tall haughty faeries, as handsome as sin, were decked out in pirate's garb of capes, jackets, blousy shirts, bright sashes, and high boots. Only the capes were tattered and flowing, the blousy shirts were diaphanous, and the wide sleeves of their jackets hung down like the specter's shroud. The whole ensemble looked not so much like pirates as masqueraders at an eerie Venetian ball impersonating pirates.

On the side of the hull, scripted in flowery loops, was *The Mangled Treasure.*

Red Caps threw down copper hooks, green with patina, that caught on a tree and a bicycle rack.

"Heave! Heave!" the crew shouted harshly. Three large, burly trolls winched the ship down to the ground. The tree swayed wildly. Up top, Red Caps and pixies reefed the mainsail and the foresail. With a rusty creak, the stern of the ship opened outward, descending until it touched the ground to form a ramp.

The harsh crack of a whip made Clara jump. A huge creature, muscle-bound and awkward, stumbled forward; one big red eye peered out from the middle of its head. It was bound in chains. A huge spiked bronze collar surrounded its neck, and similar rings encircled each wrist and each ankle. The greenish chains were held by many Red Caps, each anchored by a troll.

That was a Cyclops, from Greek mythology! What was it doing on a ship run by nightmares out of the Brothers Grimm?

The horrible creature with the ghoulish, mouthless face held the whip. It drove the Cyclops down the ramp. Shuffling slowly, the one-eyed brute moved to the red Chevy parked by itself and secured the vehicle with the hooks. Then it shuffled up the ramp again, grunting under the onslaught of lashes when it paused, and began turning a crank. Slowly, with jerks and stops, the car was winched up onto the deck.

Then the captain gave the signal. An unseen mechanism hoisted up the stern ramp and the faery square-rigger floated eerily upward. Atop, the pixies raised the sails, and the ship shot off over the buildings, straight up into the cloudy night sky.

Clara lowered her binoculars and stared after the departing faerie ship, her body trembling. That detective guy had been right. She owed him an apology.

She stared after the ship for a long time, fear warring with determination. Then she stood up, shook herself, and headed across town to wait for the library to open.

#

By the time Clara scrunched down on the floor of her rental car and spread the blanket over her head, it was already dark. It was cold down here and the rug smelled faintly of vomit; she had not thought to check that when she rented the vehicle.

She rested her head against her old gym bag—from the days when she had time for things like going to the gym. The bag was stuffed with the goodies she had bought after her trip to the library, things the books at the library had suggested she might need. Of course, the gym bag did not smell that great either, but even old musty sweat was preferable to vomit.

As she waited in the dark, under the blanket, in the chilly, smelly car, she prayed. Her great faith in God had never wavered, not through all the curve-balls life had thrown her. She just no longer trusted that God would answer her prayers. Still, it did no harm to ask him. He was a God of Mercy, maybe he would take pity on her plight.

More likely, of course, he was laughing his Divine rear off.

The car lurched and bumped. Clara's stomach tensed. Was it them? Maybe her prayers had been heard after all.

She grabbed her gym bag tight with one hand and braced herself against the seat with the other. There was a moment of stillness accompanied by a low clanking sound. Then the car began to move. As it swayed in the air, Clara snorted with sad amusement: first prayer answered in eight years, and God picks her request to be kidnapped by faery pirates.

#

Clara lay very still, listening for the sound of retreating feet. The ride on the faery square-rigger took about half an hour, according to her cell phone. Then the car had been lowered again into its current location. There had been some banging around, some muffled voices, and a loud scraping sound. Then everything went quiet.

Very slowly, Clara pushed the blanket aside and sat up. She crawled onto the back seat and peered through the window. Another car sat next to hers, and then another and another and another. She sat up higher and peered farther. No one seemed to be about. Opening the door, she climbed out and shimmied up on to the roof of the rental, shading her eyes to help her see in the pale moonlight.

There were cars as far as she could see.

The sea of cars spread out from her current position in all directions except to the left, where a tall building stood. In the other direction, toward the edge of her field of vision, she saw a couple of boats standing among the vehicles. To the right of that, near what might be a road, was that... a plane?

How would she ever find Mr. Spaghetti?

Jumping down, Clara gave the rental car a fond goodbye pat. With the loss of this car went her very last credit card, the one she had been keeping for emergencies, in case one of the kids got really sick and needed more doctoring than their mother could provide.

She shrugged and threw the strap of the gym bag over her shoulder. No point crying over spilled milk, after all, or spilled credit. No point in berating herself for not thinking to take one of the kids' backpacks instead of a bag that merely has a strap, either. She just hoped she would not have to run. Otherwise, her carefully compiled gear was a going to give her a spanking with every step.

She crept quietly forward, peering into each car as she went, shivering a little despite her inside-out sweatshirt—that was one of the tricks she had picked up during her time in the library. Wearing your clothes inside out was supposed to keep Faeries at bay. From time to time, she stopped and listened, but she could hear nothing except the hum of a freeway in the distance. She soon realized that her current efforts were futile. The gibbous moon was not bright enough to let her distinguish the details of individual cars at a distance. There was no way to spot her car from afar and far, far too many cars to search individually.

Setting off for the huge building she had glimpsed to the left, Clara swore solemnly that if she ever got her car back, she would buy one of those little Disney figures at Smarty-Mart that snapped onto the antenna to help you find your car in a crowded parking lot. A new electronic opener—something she could point and click, and her car would light up—would be even better, but those cost a pretty penny. More pennies than were in her piggy bank.

#

The bay door led into some kind of warehouse or factory. She could not see much, stumbling around in the dark, but it must have been a large place, because every object she accidentally knocked or kicked echoed eerily. She needed to find a light switch. She flicked her gym bag in annoyance and snorted. All this clever gear, and she had not thought to bring a flashlight. And her piece-of-crap pay-as-you-go cellphone didn't have a large enough screen to illuminate anything but her foot.

Of course, in her defense, it had been two o'clock in the afternoon when she came up with this plan. Only she had not been able to find anyone who would babysit her kids while they were awake. So she had been forced to wait until after bedtime. Even so, she had been forced to promise to do her sister's laundry for a month. Candice was smart enough to know that a night without Mr. Spaghetti would be no picnic.

After bashing her head on some hanging thingamajig, Clara finally found a door leading to another room. On the far side of the door, she found a light switch, only now she no longer needed it.

Before her stretched a foundry. It was dimly lit, but the bright orangey glow of molten metal illuminated the vast area, making it look like a nightmare about the fourth circle of Hell. The place smelled of hot metal and was warm, a welcome change from the chill of the night. Clara moved forward cautiously, glad she had paused before flicking the switch. She was obscured by shadows that would have vanished had she blunderingly flicked on a new light source.

From her position, she could not see the workforce. They must be too small relative to the gigantic cylindrical vats. However, workforce there must have been, because huge cranes were lowering cars—full size sedans and SUVs—into the molten vats. Far above the factory floor, a wooden command center hung out over the work area, supported by buttresses. Clara stopped beneath it and gave the structure the Hairy Eye. Who would be kooky enough to use burnable materials, instead of steel or glass, in an environment filled with fiery sparks?

Faeries, of course, who cannot touch cold iron—and apparently not hot iron either.

If the faerie overlords were not willing to come onto the factory floor, what did the workforce consist of? More enslaved Cyclopses?

With a loud grinding creak, one of the vats tipped. A stream of hot yellow liquid poured into some kind of long trough, illuminating more of the building. Shadows fled from the corner around her. Clara saw something pale dangling on the wall to her right. She moved to investigate.

"Dear God!" She pressed her hand against her mouth, hard.

Hanging suspended by a rope was the detective who had questioned her the previous day, the one who had promised to get her car back. He hung by his wrists, dangling above a circle of toadstools that grew directly from the cement. His face had been beaten. He had a black eye and an ugly purple and greenish bruise on one cheek. He did not seem to be breathing. "Is he... are you dead?"

"Nah, it's okay, ma'am." The voice came from some place to the left of the body. It sounded as if a pair of cymbals had been granted a voice and were speaking with a Bronx accent. "That's just my body. Normally, I stay in there. I kinda got out of it, on account as I did not like the way they was treating it."

"What... what are you?" Clara's hand was already in the gym bag, reaching around for some kind of weapon. She pulled something out at random and found herself holding a bell and a carton of salt. Would that work? The fairytales had not been very specific on the subject of what worked on who.

"Ever read The Tempest, by that Speareshaker guy?" His voice now issued from the air above the closest point of the toadstool circle When Clara nodded, he continued. "Remember Ariel? Well, I'm his... you'd call it a brother. Only I spend my time in this body here, on account of how Mr. Prospero wants me to be able to help you humans. He's the one who decided I was to be a detective. Name is Mab, by the way."

"Mab?" Clara looked to and fro, but could see no sign of the speaker, which made sense, she supposed, if he was some kind of spirit of air. She crossed her arms. "I thought that was the Faerie Queen's name?"

"Nah, her name was Maeve. Spencer got a little confused."

"I see. Can I get you down?" Clara took a step forward, eyeing the toadstools dubiously. "I brought some herbicide."

"Herbicide? Clever! A girl after my own heart. You'll probably need it, but don't use it here. There are other spells, you might get hurt."

"What can I do?"

The voice was silent for a moment. Then, with a sigh, he said, "Ma'am, I'm going to ask you a favor. I realize you might not be able to grant it, but I... I gotta ask."

"Go ahead," Clara eyed the air suspiciously. "Worst I can do is say no."

"In order to get anything out of here, you're going to have to face the faeries. Faeries don't got free will—well not in the way that a creature with a soul does. They are constrained to obey certain rules."

"Like them leaving a poor soul alone if his clothes are inside out, or not crossing a circle of salt?" Clara asked. What had seemed warm when she first stepped in from outside was now growing uncomfortably hot. She wiped sweat from her brow.

"Right! And they have to stick to the rules under which they operate, whether they like it or not. And they're tricky. Comes from having no hope of Heaven, you know; no reason to behave. If you survive whatever they throw at you, they'll let you pick one thing to take away with you. Pick me."

Clara drew her head back and stared at him like he was bonkers. "Pick you, not my car with Mr. Spaghetti?"

"Pick me, ma'am, cause once I get out of here, I can shut this place down. Shut it down forever. But... let's just say I can put everything back where it goes—I could do it now, if I could get to my danged cell phone, but I can't work it in this form, and you can't cross the magic circle to get it for me."

Mab's voice became more serious. "If you pick something else, ma'am you'll get to leave with it, but everything else will stay here. Until... some other mortal happens upon me, I guess. I could be here a very long time. Not that that's your problem."

"What's the number? I could call them." Clara offered, pulling out her phone.

The voice sounded truly embarrassed. "No one commits numbers to memory any more."

Clara put her hands on her hips and snorted. "You think that's going to be hard, Detective Mab. On one hand, I get a doll or a car. On the other hand, I get the doll, my car, the rental, and I save you, another human be... another living being. And you think I'm going to find this decision hard?" She waggled her head at him. "You have another thing coming."

The detective's voice was low and sad. "Ma'am, you have no idea. If you chose to ask for me, I swear I will do everything in my power to return... everything here that is yours. But if you do not, I'll understand. Mortals can only bear so much."

"You're crazy," Clara took a step back, unnerved. "You may have believed me and be an airy spirit without a body and all, but you're still as kooky as a... kooky thing!"

"Just sayin', ma'am. That's all," replied the detective.

Clara held up her hand, as if she were saying the Pledge of Allegiance. "I give you my solemn word I will ask for you. There. How's that! I am a woman of integrity. I. Do. Not. Break. My. Word."

"You shouldn't have done that, ma'am... but thank you."

#

She slipped around the wall and was about to head up the stairs to the command room when she saw it. Her car! It sitting in the line of cars waiting to be turned into slag. Clara flew down the stairs that led to the waiting area. She hunkered down and ran between the vehicles like a spy in the movies. Reaching hers, she fumbled with her keys, breathing hard. Then, she had the door open.

A lunge into the back, and Mr. Spaghetti was in her hands!

Clara shut the door and sat down, leaning against the tires of the next car over, a huge green van. She hugged the stupid, tattered rag-doll to her chest, its fingerprint-stained, spaghetti-like hair flopped against her shoulder.

"You caused me a whole whopper of trouble, Buddy O!" she whispered to the silly thing. "I don't know what my son sees in you, but he loves you."

But that was the way of love, was it not? Heck, she would probably feel the same way about whatever goofy boy Sari eventually picked for a husband.

She blew her nose on an old tissue she found in her pocket and toyed with her cell phone as she thought about calling home to check on the kids. Reluctantly, she decided not to. The last thing Candice needed was for the phone to wake Sammy.

He had cried himself to sleep, the poor baby.

She felt bad about imposing upon her sister, who had her own family to worry about. Back when Sari was little, she would have asked her neighbor. That neighbor no longer talked to her, though, ever since Sammy peed on their front door. Clara tried to reprimand him at the time, to show that she understood their concern, but Sammy just laughed, his white teeth flashing in his silly dark head.

Clara could call him silly, because she had earned the right through sweat and tears, but the Lord help anyone else who dared call her son names!

She did not know if the neighbors blamed Sammy for urinating with malicious intent or blamed her for letting him out to play—for Pete's sake, she could not keep an eye on him every single minute! She was only human!—either way, they just had not understood.

Of course, her sister's children had a daddy to watch them when their mama was out; so maybe she should not feel so bad about imposing on Candi.

146

Clara gave the rag doll a last fierce hug and shoved it in her bag. She wiped the sweat from her face again. What to do now? If it were not for the detective, she would just leave now. Forget the car, forget that she had ever seen anything like this. Just get the doll back to Sammy and life could go back to normal... without a car or a credit card. But she felt bad just abandoning the guy. Maybe she should try the herbicide on the toadstools after all.

Wiping a stray tear from her eye that had crept out when she was hugging the doll, she rose to her feet. As she did so, she glanced toward the factory floor.

Where had all the children come from?

Clara's feet did not move toward the door. Instead, they crept closer to the factory floor.

It was like walking into a Dickensian nightmare. Children, from tiny three year olds to burly teens, worked the factory, moving levers, throwing switches, changing the molds into which the molten metal poured. Dirty children, dressed in rags, with bruises and open sores. Sweaty children, working in all that heat. Dull-eyed children, who went through their routines without any sign of that spark that made a child well... a child.

Human children. Enslaved by faeries. Here in the modern day, in the country of freedom!

In all her years of medical school and ER work, Clara had never chucked her cookies. She had been proud of that. Her Stomach of Iron failed her now. She vomited behind the tire of a white BMW. Crouching down, she grabbed her knees and stayed there until her legs stopped shaking. Then, slowly she stood up and made herself look again.

Children. Little children, like Sammy. Like Sari. One of the little dark boys even reminded her of Sammy.

147

Despite the heat, an icy, cold chill traveled own her spine.

No, not reminded her—this boy looked like Sammy. Exactly like Sammy. Except, he looked like what Sammy would look if he were an ordinary child— without that sometimes stupid, sometimes benefic expression the real Sammy usually wore. Like what Sammy looked like when he concentrated hard, and you could not tell that there was anything amiss with him. Like what Sammy would look like with a festering wound on his cheek and forehead.

That boy out there, with burn marks on his wrist where molten sparks had caught him—the bastards did not even give the children leather gloves—looked *exactly* like her son.

How could that be?

Clara examined the rest of the children she could see. Her heart nearly stopped. There! That little girl was a splitting image of Jillian, the sole little girl in the ABA program at Sammy's school. And behind the giant crane! The boy who was missing an arm. He looked like the twin brother of Nicholas, from that Special Need's exercise class she used to drag Sammy to.

Slowly, her legs gave way. Clara sank to the cold cement floor and bowed her head.

She knew how it could be. She had only just read all those faeries stories.

Hot tears splashed from her cheeks to the floor. Her life, her wonderful career, the lives she might have saved, the husband she had—yes, she would admit it now, she had loved Stan before it all went wrong, and the coward ran out on her—all thrown away so she could raise an faerie imposture, who had been left in place of her real son.

Her Sammy was a changeling.

Now that she knew, here life finally made sense. Laughing in the face of discipline. Weird behaviors. Lack of empathy with human beings. Was that so different from laughing at funerals and the other bizarre things faeries were wont to do in tales?

And modern chemicals? Bright lights? Of course, her son could not tolerate them! He was a freaking faery! In retrospect, she wondered why she had not figured it out sooner.

Were they all changelings? Over a million autistic children in America alone. Had they all been stolen by faeries?

She thought of her friend Jenna, patiently enduring the screaming and fits of her three autistic boys. She thought of Martha, who spent her days driving from one doctor to another, determined to find the illusive missing cure. She thought of Mrs. O'Conner, whose daughter had bugged out, leaving her to raise her two autistic grandchildren.

All these women, all that labor and love, wasted on changelings —while their own children suffered as slaves.

"Samuel!" she took off at a run, sprinting across the factory floor. "Samuel!"

The little boy turned as she approached. His eyes grew large. Staring up at her in wonder, he asked in a small voice. "Are you... my mama?"

Clara grabbed him and clasped him to her heart. "I am! I am your mama! And I'm never going to leave you again!"

She knelt and hugged him, her missing son, her long lost beloved child. He smelt like metal fumes and smoke, but under that was a scent that reminded her of hugging Sari. This little boy smelt like her daughter! Any doubts Clara might have had evaporated. The two of them hugged and cried and cried and cried.

149

A scrabbling noise startled Clara, just as a Red Cap lunged for her. Screaming, Clara threw her body between the Red Cap and her son. Frantically, she stuck her hand into the gym bag, feeling around for something of use. The Red Cap let out a squeal of frustration. His hands clawed at her but did not touch her.

Her clothes! The inside-out clothes! They had worked! Losing no time, Clara grabbed her son, pulled off his soiled shirt, and turned it inside out. Putting it on him again, she took off, sprinting toward the cars and the stairs and door out beyond.

More Red Caps appeared. One wore a cutlass. One swung a copper rope. Another held two wooden belaying pins like daggers. Soon three chased her, then four. As she neared the automobiles, she saw a fifth Red Cap standing straight ahead of her, grinning. Clara ground to a stop, hugging her boy tight. She had deliberately looked up Red Caps in the library. What had that big black book claimed countered them? She rooted around in her bag for her cheat sheet.

Oh, right! Bible verses. Made them stop and loose a tooth or some such rot. Clara blurted out the only Bible passage she could bring to mind.

"Give us this day our daily bread!"

The five advancing Red Caps stopped cold. Moaning, they grabbed their jaws and writhed. A moment later, a tooth popped from each of their mouths. The teeth shot across the room, bouncing off of the floor and ricocheting off of vats. From the additional moans and pings she heard beyond her field of vision, she assumed more Red Caps had been on the way.

During all this, Clara had not been idle. She grabbed the Morton carton and spun in a circle, letting the salt pour out liberally. Then, she spun around again, to make sure she had not missed a spot. She had to pour salt on the two gaps she found, but finally she had a closed circle.

The Red Caps rushed up and crowded around the circle. They were short, bearded men in dark sailor's suits, wearing red sailor's caps and each missing a tooth. They shuffled around the circumference, as if searching for a weakness.

"Hey, little men?" Clara called. When they gathered around to hear her, she shouted, "Boo!" and gave them the Hairy Eye, the real deal, with the full force of her scorn.

The Red Caps scattered like leaves before a leaf blower.

"Now that's how it's supposed to work!" Clara hooted triumphantly, her confidence returned. "God only knows what was up with that detective. He didn't even blink!"

From the far side of the factory came a curtain of sparkling lights. This glittering pixy dust sprinkled like rain onto any children that got in its way. These children slowed and stood still. Some staring blankly, others slumping and falling to the ground, asleep. Clara grabbed her frightened son close and murmured, "Salt, don't fail me now!"

As the curtain of sleepy sand approached, Clara saw that a platoon of pixies flew above, dropping the pixy dust from little pouches they carried on their belts. The pixies flew directly toward her. There was nowhere to run. Clara gritted her teeth and stood tall.

The glittering wall of golden dust struck the circle of salt and curved, until Clara and Samuel seemed to be surrounded by a semi-circular curtain of shimmering light. But neither the pixies nor the dust crossed the salt.

"Hot dang!" Clara grinned widely. "Those books at the library *rock*!"

151

The pixy dust hung in the air for a little while, like motes in a beam of light, then it slowly sank to the ground, forming a sparkly, golden semi-circle around her white circle.

Samuel looked up from where Clara had pushed him against her body, his eyes wide. "What happens now, Mama?"

"Don't know, Pumpkin. We wait."

"I'm scared, Mama."

"I'm here with you, Baby." She smoothed his curly hair. "I'm not gonna leave you!"

A door opened in the wooden command center, and the captain of *The Mangled Treasure* emerged. He began floating down. Clara scowled. The ship's name had seemed kind of amusing when she read it in the park. It did not seem amusing now.

The captain was tall and fae, with silver-dark eyes and pale translucent skin. His long coat fluttered about him like wings as he descended. His features were godlike and easy on the eye; his expression was distant and cruel. As he came closer, Clara saw that the captain had lost a limb at the knee. In its place was a silver peg leg inscribed with Celtic knotwork.

A tiny pixy sat on his shoulder. The pixy, too, was in pirate garb: tri-corned hat, blousy white shirt, black, half-open vest, red sash, blue pantaloons, black boots and a copper cutlass—the whole works.

"What you think you doin'?" Clara always reverted to the language of her youth when she got really angry. "Takin' advantage of these po', defenseless children?"

The captain smiled. His teeth were all sharp; two were made of silver. "My! Aren't you a feisty one, me Beauty! But yer days of wreaking havoc here are over. Hand over the boy and go, before we find more appealing uses for 'ye. Arrgh!"

He spoke like a pirate using all the correct words and intonations, but his voice was languid and insolent, entirely out of keeping with his words. It was creepy.

"Appeal this, you POS!" Clara snarled, as she rooted around in the gym bag. Lord, she had better get out more. She had spent so much time around children, she had forgotten how to swear properly. "You let these children go, or you're going to be sorry you ever drew air!"

"Begging your pardon, me Beauty, but are ye referring to me crew?" The captain gestured lazily toward the factory floor. His fingernails were long and crowned with slender caps from which long needles protruded. He saw her looking and held them up, wiggling them, "The better to claw out the eyes of disrespectful ship hands," adding languidly, "Arrgh."

"Arrgh!" growled the pixy on his shoulder. "Those scurvy louts!"

"They are CHILDREN!" Clara shouted. "They are supposed to be out playing and running around."

"On the contrary," the faery pirate captain drawled. "When children are left to their own devices, they are prone to cause havoc. We put a stop to that." He leaned back his head and stroked his non-existent beard with a black-gloved hand. Airily, he added, "Me thinks ye should be thankin' us for the service!"

"Arrgh!" repeated the pixy on his shoulder. "Otherwise, you'd be swabbing up the mess."

Clara glared at the little bugger. What was he supposed to be, the parrot?

"I ain't even dignifying that with a comment," she grumbled, as she searched her bag.

Her hand came away with a handful of powdered chalk and a pile of red thread. She threw the stuff down with a grunt of disgust. They were no use! She plunged her hand back into the bag again. It had to be here somewhere!

"These wee ones are our weaponsmiths. They make pistols and spears, for use against our enemies, the Unseelie Court. Or are we the Unseelie Court?" The captain cocked his head to address the pixy. "So hard to keep these trivialities straight. The Servelings make weapons now. When they get bigger, we give into their pathetic mewling and let them wield the things. They're given the honor of cutting down our enemies, Arrgh! Fine bully boys, they make, all hot with anger. We cannot make or hold iron weapons ourselves, of course."

"Arrgh!" declared the pixy. "Melts us like slag." It grinned nastily. "Melts our enemies like slag, too, and they don't got themselves a Serveling army!"

"Servelings! The word you are looking for is *slave!*" Clara spat. "You've enslaved children to make weapons?"

The captain of the *Mangled Treasure* chuckled deeply. "Aye, the blackbirdy has spunk, do she not? Look at her bristle like a vixen defending her kit. If we had mothers, lads, we would know how mothers get, wouldn't we?"

There was muttering laughter from the redcap pirates, answered by tinkling giggles from the little floating pixies. Clara glanced around, unnerved. She had not realized they had an audience.

The captain continued, "Besides, me fierce Beauty, the little powder-monkeys do more than just forge weapons. Some are lucky enough to become cabin boys, or personal servants to other fae. They serve many uses, quite versatile, really."

"Very useful, Arrgh!" the pixy leered, "Especially the saucy little wenches!"

"If they are useful," Clara asked through clenched teeth, "why do you treat them so badly?"

"'Treat them badly?'" The captain turned to regard the children, puzzled. "I see no harm upon them. They are given food, water, and a mat to sleep upon, same as any crewman. What more would ye have us do?"

Clara glared at him, but the captain merely looked confused. Her blood ran cold. Great Mother of Heaven, he was serious. The faeries were so callous, so alien to human kind, they did not even know the children were being harmed.

Finally! Clara's shaking hand—shaking more with wrath than fear now—closed upon her *piece de resistance*. She held it tightly, but did not pull it from the gym bag yet.

"Listen here, Faery-face, I'm leaving and I'm taking my son!" she declared.

"Arrgh! I think not. Pirates never relinquish their loot," The faery pirate smiled, showing his sharpened silver teeth. "However, Ancient Law, far older than the ways of pirates, require that we must let ye go—with a single object of yer choice—if you can successfully answer a riddle."

"Listen here, you Jack Sparrow wanna-be!" Clara drew the sawed off shotgun from her gym bag and aimed it at the faery captain. "I ain't playing any of your pixy games! I am a lady of principle! I. Do. Not. Make. Deals. With. Slavers."

"I fear ye have no choice, me Saucy Lass, yer in our territory now. Our territory, our rules!" The captain seemed totally unworried. Behind her the Red Caps and trolls cheered loudly.

"See this shotgun?" Clara trained it on the faery pirate captain's chest. "It's packed with rock salt and iron filings. Iron hurts you guys, doesn't it? Of course it does, or you wouldn't bother kidnapping helpless babies! Do you know what these filings are gonna do to you when they hit you? Suppurating lung wounds. Ripped aorta. Perforated stomach wall.

"Don't you mess with no MD, Punks!" Clara chortled, jabbing the gun at him. "When it comes to knowing how to hurt, we can open up a whole can of whup on your sorry ass!"

"Arrgh! Tradition requires that we..." the faery pirate captain began.

Clara aimed the gun at his head and set her feet.

"Or we can declare the riddle answered and move on," the faery captain amended. "Oh, very well, ye may ask for one thing, and one thing alone to take away with ye. Anything ye likes out of our booty. Cars. Pieces of eight. Magic rings. Whatsoever ye please."

Clara opened her mouth to tell them that it was sure as Hell going to be her son. Only she stopped. Behind her, laboring in the factory, were the other children, hundreds of other children, thousands of other children.

"What if I want to take them all?" She asked. "Do you need me to remind you of what is gonna happen to you and your punk pixy mini-me if I pull this trigger?"

"Now don't do anything hasty, Me Feisty One!" The captain urged. "We of the Old Lineage are bound by yer circle, but them thar human Servelings are not. Children love shooting pistols, ye know, and we have many here. What a tragedy t'would be if ye and yer little boy were gunned down by yer own kind. Poets would write ballads about it.".

"Cut the act!" Clara snarled. "You can't possibly really talk like a pirate."

"Aye, most likely not, me Beauty, but you wouldn't want to see me out O' my pirate guise. I give you me word on that!"

The captain began to grow, taller and darker. Shadows gathered about him like a shroud. Antlers sprouted from his brow, and his eyes began to glow with a reddish light. Behind her, Clara could hear the Red Caps and trolls stealthily retreating. The little pixy on his shoulder gave a cry of horror and fled.

"You would not like me without my pirate guise, Creature who smells of mortal blood," came the eerie, rasping words.

"Okay, okay! Do the pirate thing already!" Clara cried out, her voice shrill.

All that bulk and shadow might be a posturing, especially if he still could not get through the circle of salt, but she would not take any chances. Besides that big, black, glowing-eyes, horned thingy gave her the creeps!

The captain shrank again and donned his fallen tri-corner hat. "Tis all right, me Hearties. Yer captain has returned. Fer the moment, anyways."

There was a hearty cheer, and the Red Caps, trolls, and pixies slowly came back. The little one circled cautiously two or three times before landing again on the captain's shoulder.

"All right, me Hearties!" it sang out. "The captain won't eat us today!"

The captain turned and leered at Clara. "What be yer decision, me Beauty?"

Clara paused, torn. She looked across the factory floor at all the other little damaged souls. Someone else would have to rescue them. Or maybe she could come back with the police. If the police believed her. If they knew enough to use chalk circles and not just get enchanted.

On the other hand, what if this Mab person could not actually help? What if his promise was a trap?

Clara closed her eyes and prayed. Then, she knelt beside her son. "Samuel, honey. I love you more than air itself. But I promised someone who can save all the children that I would ask the faeries to let me take him out with me. It's very important to keep your word, and we want to save all your friends. I'm going to have to leave you here and come back for you. Is that okay?"

In the best of worlds, Samuel would have smiled at her and said, "That's all right, Mama." But Clara's life had never been in the best of worlds.

Samuel's bottom lip began to quiver, the way her daughter Sari's did when she was about to cry. He grabbed her leg with both hands and held on.

"No! Mama, no! What about your promise to me?" he cried, his voice heart-piercingly shrill. "You told me you would never leave me again! Mama! They hurt me here, Mama! Don't leave! Don't leave me!"

Clara felt as if she had been pierced to the very center of her soul. If someone had shoved a hot poker through her spine and into her heart, it could not have hurt as much as this.

But when the leering faery captain insisted and she, herself, tore her son from her leg and left him, weeping, on the factory floor— that hurt more.

#

Outside on the chilly street, Clara knelt beneath a street lamp, pounding her fists on the pavement and weeping. Detective Mab walked up beside her. He looked bruised and beaten.

"Blow me to the North Pole, you chose me!" he whistled. He looked stunned.

He pulled out his cell phone. Clara shook her head, whipping her slender braids about yet again. She was sitting next to an airy spirit who was using a cell phone. What had the world come to?

"What happens now?" she asked dully when he folded his phone again.

"We wait for the cavalry."

"The cavalry?"

"The *Orbis Suleimani*," he growled.

"The Circle of Solomon?" Clara translated. She had taken Latin to help her with her medical work.

"Organization set up by King Solomon to protect humans from the supernatural." Mab explained. "Nowadays, Mr. Prospero's in charge. We've been looking for these pirate jokers for a long time, but we were having trouble locating 'em." A look of disgust came over Mab's features. "Stealing from humans! Enslaving children! Those punks had to go down!"

"They can't be responsible for all autistic children. There weren't enough children there," Clara murmured, more to herself.

Mab looked grim. "They aren't the only ring of slavers, ma'am, but we'll get 'em. We'll get 'em all!"

"Why children?" Her voice sounded unnaturally shrill. "Why not just kidnap adults? Adults would be infinitely more useful for fighting a war."

Mab shrugged. "One of those rules, like why they can't cross salt. They are allowed to take children before their second birthday. After that, all sorts of restrictions kick in. Free will, and all that."

"How long has this been going on?" Clara asked. "Them stealing so many children?"

Mab shrugged both shoulders. "Don't rightly know, ma'am, but I can hazard a guess that it's probably a modern thing. It's only recently, in this age of so-called science, that people have stopped following the old ways, protecting their thresholds, and doing the other things that would keep the faerie folk away. Apparently, the faeries figured this out, too."

Ahead, perhaps a dozen dark figures carrying tall staffs approached the factory building. Just before the door, they halted. Soon, they were joined by more figures in wide hoods and long flowing cloaks. When what appeared to Clara to be a small army of SCA members had assembled, they moved, streaming into the building. Clara lowered her head and prayed that, whatever happened, no one would hurt the children.

As she glanced up again, her gaze fell on the gym bag. Mr. Spaghetti's head stuck out of the open top. Clara grabbed the doll and hugged it. Then she flung it away from her.

Mab raised an eyebrow. He walked over and picked up the discarded rag doll, examining it front and back. "Begging your pardon, ma'am, but isn't that what you came here to find?"

Clara glared at him and snarled. "My life, my health, my marriage, all the sacrifices I made—I thought I was doing the right thing! The good thing! But that... monster is not my son, not even a human being. Just some kind of..." tears threatened to spill over her lashes again, "some kind of soulless monster."

It was the pain, the humiliation, of not having noticed that hurt the most –of having loved him so much. It was worse, even, than having wasted her beauty and her youth on Stan.

Mab took off his hand. "Ma'am, you must be a praying woman."

Clara glared at him suspiciously. "What makes you say that?"

"Cause only the Almighty could arrange a coincidence like this one. Less than a dozen beings on this world who could tell you what I'm about to say, and only one of those who has actually been through it happens to be me." He paused and pushed up the brim of his hat. "Before I go on, let me ask you—truthfully, using your own judgment. Do you really believe your son—your other son, I mean, Sammy, I think you call him—has no soul?"

Clara closed eyes and pictured the thing she used to think of as her son—that moaning, bobbing freak who had broken her nose. But what she saw in her mind's eye was not the screaming, thrashing Sammy, but his beneficent smile, that open clear look in his eyes—like gazing into the eye of an angel.

Suddenly, Clara knew, from the crown of her head to the bottoms of her sneakers, that Sammy had a soul. She had seen that soul gazing back at her. Sammy might not be the son she had given birth to, but he loved her!

Wordlessly, Clara nodded. Somehow, the detective seemed to know what she meant.

"You clearly know something about faeries. Have you ever come upon the story of St. Patrick and the mermaid?" asked Mab.

Clara shook head.

"Well, the short version is that St. Patrick once got a mermaid a soul. It can happen. Mr. Prospero, my boss, he investigated it. Found out that the easiest way to grant a supernatural creature a soul is to put it in a human body and let 'em live with humans, interact and communicate with humans, learn decency and love.

"Ma'am," Mab put his hat back on and handed her Mr. Spaghetti. "Before Mr. Prospero gave me this body, I was as soulless as the rest of my fellow airy spirits. But then I started hanging out with

Mr. Prospero's daughter, Miss Miranda—you may remember her from the play— and learning stuff about humans. To make a long story short, I came upon this little silver star that only people with souls could hold... and it didn't fall through my hand and it didn't burn me. I held it just like any other human... I'd won me a soul!

Clara clenched the doll. "Wait. Sammy might not have had a soul when I got him, but he might have one now?"

Mab stuck his hands in the pocket of his trench coat. "Bodies change the way we think. Faeries going into a child's body becomes a child the same way immortal souls conceived by the Almighty sent into a child's body becomes a child. That faery who impersonated your son had never known motherly love. He'd never known courage or sacrifice or any of those things you've been doing for him. Do you think soullessness can hold out against the power of a Mother's Love?"

Clara lifted her chin. "You mean, in return for giving up my cushy life and the lives I might have saved... I helped a soulless creature gain a soul?"

"Exactly, ma'am."

Clara stood there, flabbergasted. "Did... did the faeries do this on purpose? Is that why they left us changelings?"

Mab shook his head. "Nope. They haven't got a clue. Don't know it happens."

"But what... what is a soul, Mab?"

Mab gave a tired, weathered smile. "The key to the Pearly Gates, ma'am. That little boy you're raising? The one who loves that goofy rag-doll you're strangling?" Mab looked her straight in the eye. "Thanks to you, the gates of Heaven just opened for him."

#

Children began to pour out of the building into the faint moonlight. Clara saw Samuel right away. He paused, looking for her, and then came running as fast as his feet could go. Clara's heart leapt. She had feared he would never trust her again. She ran to him, lifted him up, and swung him around in the air. He laughed, but hearing it squeezed Clara's heart, it was a hesitant, rusty sound, a sound a child might make if he had never laughed before.

Children mulled everywhere, shivering in the chilled night. In the midst of them, Clara saw the Cyclops. His collar still on his neck, and his copper chains dragging behind him. He stopped and stood blinking his single red eye, as he gazed at the street around him. Then a tall figure carrying a staff came and gestured for the creature to follow him.

Mab came over to join her. Clara hugged Samuel fiercely, holding him to her chest, and surveyed the crowd. There had to be thousands of children here.

"How is anyone ever going to find their parents?" she mused.

Mab rotated his shoulders. "Not sure how I'd do it myself, but I know a fella who might be able to help. He's got a list with their names on it, watches 'em when they're naughty and nice. Maybe he could deliver them on his rounds this year, like Christmas presents."

"Santa's real, too," Clara gave a short laugh. "Lordy, That's too much for me! I'm taking my son and going home!"

#

So, now Clara had three children. She had to change her real son's name. Could not have two boys in the house both called Samuel, and it made sense to change the name of the one who had only just learned he was a Samuel. She called him Stanley, she thought his good-for-nothing father would have liked that.

163

It was not an easy life, but Clara would not have traded it for anything—not even to have been the head ER physician at Mercy Hospital, married to the most handsome man in the county.

She kept an eye on the news, tracking the stories about the "foundlings." Children arrived in homes far and wide—apparently these *Orbis Suleiman* guys made the faeries give back all their changelings, all over the world.

It was not an easy time. These battered children went to homes that were already dealing with problems. Some families had two or three such children. Her friend Jenna was suddenly the mother of six!

Some families rejected the new children, who were then shunted off into the foster system. Some rejected their changeling in favor of their flesh and blood. But, for the most part, they did what families always have done since the dawn of time, they made do. They found room. They loved them all.

In America alone, over a million faeries had gained souls.

About the Author

L. Jagi Lamplighter is the author of the YA fantasy: *The Unexpected Enlightenment of Rachel Griffin*. She is also the author of the Prospero's Daughter series: *Prospero Lost, Prospero In Hell*, and *Prospero Regained*. She has published numerous articles on Japanese animation and appears in several short story anthologies, including *Best Of Dreams Of Decadence, No Longer Dreams, Coliseum Morpheuon, Bad-Ass Faeries Anthologies* (where she is also an assistant editor) and the Science Fiction Book Club's *Don't Open This Book*.

When not writing, she switches to her secret identity as wife and stay-home mom in Centreville, VA, where she lives with her dashing husband, author John C. Wright, and their four darling children, Orville, Ping-Ping Eve, Roland Wilbur, and Justinian Oberon.

You   can   follow   her   on   her   website http://www.ljagilamplighter.com/   ,   blog http://arhyalon.livejournal.com/ and on Twitter @lampwright4

Editor's Note: An abbreviated version of this story first appeared in *Bad Ass Fairies 2: Just Plain Bad*, published by Mundania Press in 2009

Serial

Beyond the Mist

Ben Zwycky

Chapter 8—The River

I kicked out at the cliff edge and felt some purchase, which would hopefully move me away from the rocks at the bottom of the gorge. The empty box acted as something of a sail, but before I could decide whether it was actually helping, I plunged into the water and its buoyancy wrenched it out of my hand.

The cold shock of the water made me want to gasp, but I fought the urge as I sank down to the bottom. My boots reached solid rock and I kicked myself back up to the surface, unable to see a thing. The water was relatively calm, but with a definite current. I frantically looked around for the box, then as my eyes adjusted I caught sight of a faintly glowing rectangular form about three or four metres away, the translucent plastic of the box catching what meagre starlight reached down into the gorge differently from any other object down there.

It was rocking up and down and slowly turning. I took this to mean it would soon be picked up by the stream and swept away from me, so I swam over to it as quickly as I awkwardly could in my clothes and boots, coughing out a couple of mouthfuls of water along the way. As I reached my objective in the shallow water, the light in the gorge grew brighter, illuminating the box and the sharp rocks it was caught on more clearly. I grabbed the box and looked up. The bright white crescent of Leukos, about a quarter of the diameter of Sidereos, had just appeared from behind a cloud.

The lip of the box seemed to have caught on the tip of a sharp rock, simply pressing down on my end of the box lifted it free.

Something hissed down out of the darkness and smashed into the rocks in front of me; the light was not only helping me see, but also making me a more visible target to whoever I knocked over. I lifted the box over to wherever the current looked strongest and dived on top of it, allowing myself to be swept downstream at a speed that I hoped would discourage my adversary from pursuing.

If he did follow me, I had enough distractions to fail to notice any further attempts to injure me. It was a wild ride over all sorts of stationary waves, hydraulic jumps, channel narrowings and widenings and sharp changes in the direction of the current. Almost every time I failed to anticipate a wave or change in current, or caught my foot on a stone, I would tip over into the water and bash my arm, leg, back or hip against an unforgiving obstacle. Each time I would keep a firm grip on the box and scramble back on top of it, putting its buoyant bulk between me and the next collision.

Every so often there would be a disconcerting crunch, which I hoped was stone fragments being ground against each other and not plastic being punctured. These incidents became more frequent as the gorge walls grew higher and higher, permitting less and less light into its depths.

Each impact on the same part of my body multiplied the pain.

Each climb back onto my flotation device was more tiring than the last.

The descent into deeper and deeper darkness became ever more frightening, until I began to hope that my head would take the next impact and put me out of my misery.

Just as I began to consider how to make that more likely to happen, I caught a glimpse of a shaft of light up ahead. With the way

I was being thrown about by the torrent, it was difficult to tell what it was, but as the light grew closer I realised it was the end of the gorge.

Hope gave new strength to my aching muscles and I renewed my grip on the box, watching for obstacles with newfound alertness, even anticipating a wave and keeping myself upright. The channel widened and slowed as I exited the gorge into the large natural basin that fed the four waterfalls.

I was tempted to just relax and lie down on the box, then remembered that the drop into the pool was a significant height, so I slipped off into the water, trying to slow my approach and move towards the rock outcrop that split the two central falls. The current proved too strong and I went over the centre-left fall, doing my best to fall feet first and pushing the box to my right to avoid landing on it. I plunged into the deep water and its relative calm filled me with such relief that I momentarily forgot all the pain in my body.

I drifted slowly down to the bottom, just soaking in the tranquility, looking up at the vaguely shimmering surface above me that now belonged to another, irrelevant world. Here all was beautiful, all was serene. A growing tightness in my chest reminded me that there was something this world did not have.

Air.

I kicked off the bottom and clawed my way to the surface, breathing in great gasps of cool night air, any sound I made drowned out by the roars of the nearby waterfalls. I looked around for my buoyancy aid and saw it maybe ten metres away, listing badly to one corner. I grunted in annoyance.

Definitely holed. Maybe if I flipped it over, or just get to the edge of this pool and move on...

That's when I saw the flickering glow of burning torches spread along the right-hand side of the pool. I looked the other way, and there was a similar number of lights on the other side. I was surrounded. A series of expletives ran through my mind.

Are they Apples, or one of the other tribes? Even if they were, would that be any better? Killed for abandoning the Apples or killed for being one in the first place? I'll have to try and ride further down the river.

I lay as flat as I could, floating in the water, moving slowly away from the waterfalls and towards the box to avoid attracting any attention. My boots dragged me down and it required significant effort to stay afloat with them on, but taking them off was not an option, since I would need them once I got back to dry land. I got to within five metres of the box when I heard voices at the edge of the pond and froze in place:

"What's that?"

My pulse was racing.

"Looks like a food box, and with something in it."

"Go fish it out, then."

"No need, it'll be at the outflow from the pool soon, we can hook it out as it comes past. Keep a watch out for any Apples."

The light from the two torches bobbed gently as they circled around, calling to the people on the other side to come closer and narrow the gap to prevent the prize escaping them.

Inside I wanted to scream, but I trod water as quietly as I could, working against the gentle current to put distance between myself and my faithful little vessel. I heard feet splashing in the water, narrowing the gap between the torches to two or three metres as the box accelerated towards them.

172

There's no way I can get through there unnoticed.

A corner of the box lifted and stopped its forward motion, the opposite corner sweeping around into the middle of the outflow.

"Got it! Give me a hand back to shore, will you? This thing is heavy."

The torches separated again, to a gap of six or seven metres.

That's better, just back off a little more, please.

"Hard luck, Sticky. Maybe next time," taunted one of the voices on the left.

"Hang on, it's leaking something." He opened the lid and looked inside. "Gah, it's just full of water from the river."

One of the voices on the right laughed. "Hard luck, Mudface. Maybe next time."

I saw the box being thrown down in disgust, ending up on the riverbank with its lid half on.

If I could just reach it... Come on, people, there's nothing to see here, move along.

My heart slowly sank as the torches stayed where they were. Aches and tiredness grew all over my body as I struggled to remain quiet while staying afloat. *Hang on, I'm not floating, I'm standing on an underwater rock, how did that happen?*

Then to my horror I began to see the first hints of light at the edge of the sky.

Got to risk it now.

I pushed off the rock towards the outflow channel, swimming as quietly as I could, lying back as still as possible and drifting with the current as soon as it gained strength. I tried to drift towards the left hand side of the outflow, to be within reach of the box on the shore,

173

risking a sweep with my arm to turn me around and glide me that way. I instinctively froze in place as I came alongside the nearest torchlight. By what meager flickering glimmer it gave out, it looked like it had been planted in the ground and the man nearest it was looking up the hill.

Come on, come on, there it is...

Another sweep with my right arm as I reached out for the corner of the box with my left hand, hooking my fingers to grab on to the protruding corner, but the rounded point of a shallow rock dug into my ribs and flipped me around at the last second, so my fingers bounced off the box and then I was swept past and it was out of my reach.

Damnit!

"What was that?" a voice reacted to the box rattling against its lid and my stifled grunt.

No, nothing. I winced.

"There! it's an Apple in the river, trying to get past us! Get him!"

No, no, no.

The sun peeked over the horizon and rose rapidly, revealing a short section of snaking rapids ahead of me, followed by another long still pool, with spear-wielding men spread along the banks of the river on either side.

Oh, crap.

The speed of the flow meant I was outpacing the group above me, but the downstream group started to form a human chain and spread out across the channel.

Double crap.

I looked around for a way out, but before anything occurred to me the current strengthened and I was in the rapids.

I had managed to turn myself around during the initial calm section to be floating feet first and negotiated the first obstacle comfortably, pushing away from an upcoming rock with my boots. This got me out of alignment with the flow and soon I was tumbling completely out of control, gasping for breath every time my head came up out of the water. I scrabbled at every passing rock, but my aching fingers were unable to maintain their grip. There was a brief respite and I caught a glimpse of the still pool and complete human chain awaiting me, then my feet dropped and I was dragged down under a rock by the thunderous current.

The impact with the rock forced most of the air out of my lungs and I began to panic, thrashing around with rapidly dwindling strength, but I was pinned. The panic ebbed away, replaced by a resigned sorrow.

I am so tired, so tired. Can't I just give up now?

I opened my eyes and saw what I assumed was sunlight creeping under the rock. I reached into the gap and my fingers closed around something stringlike. I pulled and found a lit beacon entangled around a small stick. Everything was going dark as I pressed the button three times. It flashed a bright blue and then everything went black.

#

I became aware of a bright warm light and a foul stench. I dared to open my eyes a crack and immediately closed them again, it was too much. I turned my head to the other side, in the process scraping my face against something rough but malleable. The light wasn't as bright that way, and I tried opening my eyes again.

I was on the left bank of a river, I assumed it was the same river, but the water was brown and seemed to be the source of the foul

175

smell. Out of the corner of my eye I could see a large clump of trees to my right, and that the beacon on its cord was still in my right hand, though its light was now switched off. I lifted my head from the polluted sand and found my entire body was aching, especially areas I had taken utterly for granted until now. With a series of grunts and groans that would make any octagenarian proud, I stood and surveyed my surroundings.

I appeared to be in the second lowest half-bowl, the last one seemed to be more extended than the rest, ending in the same vertical cliffs that surrounded the whole area, but a series of vertical rock formations were spread across its width. To my right the river meandered gently up the slope, to my left it began to descend into a deepening gorge to the lip of the last bowl, either side of the gorge being heavily forested. From what I could tell, it looked like some sort of trench had been dug just in front of the distant treeline, which was crisscrossed with sturdy branches to form an imposing fence.

I looked at the beacon in my hand, pressed the button and the little light that came on, weak as it was, filled me with a certain reassurance.

"Throws you back in the Gravity Ring, eh? What else were they wrong about? I'll be sure to keep you to hand at all times."

I gently shook and stretched various parts of my body this way and that, discovering what range of motion was relatively pain-free, then rolled up my right sleeve, revealing a patchwork of bruises. I tied the cord around my forearm and wrist so that the beacon would lie comfortably in my palm, ready to activate at a moment's notice, then unrolled my sleeve again to mask its presence.

I began up the gentle slope of the riverbank, looking for a way around the fortified woods. As the stiffness of my limbs gradually eased, the pangs of hunger and thirst became more obvious. I

176

looked back at the river, there was no way I was drinking from there, I'd have to look out for a stream. Surrounded by billow bushes, I tried snapping off one of the fronds to squeeze out the juice, but its high flexibility made that difficult. I looked around for a sharp stone to cut it with, but each one I came across had well-worn rounded edges. I hit upon the idea of biting the frond and tearing it the rest of the way, but as I bent down to sink my teeth into it, two men armed with spears appeared over the crest of the slope and immediately saw me. Both of them had blueberry markings on their left cheeks, but instead of a large empty circle with a small straight line, theirs was a small filled circle attached to a long curved line.

"Hey, you there, what are you doing?"

"I'm just looking for some food and water," I replied. "You wouldn't know where I could get some, would you?"

One lowered his spear at me. "Watch out! He's an Apple." The other one did the same. "You've got a lot of nerve coming all the way out here."

"I'm not an Apple any more, I was tricked into joining them. I want nothing to do with them and escaped at the first opportunity, jumping into a gorge in the dark and nearly drowning twice."

"We've heard that before. You try to join our tribe then betray us to your friends at the first opportunity, scout out our defences or just draw us into an ambush by your presence here. Everyone, another bit of Apple bait here! Be on the lookout for enemy forces!" A few voices beyond my line of sight acknowledged and passed on the warning.

"No, no, I don't want to join any tribe, or scout out any defences, I just want to find the lowest point in this place and get out of here."

"Let you past so you can join the Rock Eaters? No chance."

"I just said I don't want to join any tribe! What can I do to prove

177

that I'm no threat to you?"

"You can let us spill your guts out on the ground," said the one on the right, moving forward with his spear.

This is not going well. I took a nervous step back. "But if you try to kill me, I'll just disappear, be healed up and thrown back in the Gravity Ring. Then when I get out the Apples will recruit me again, I won't be able to escape and I'll be made to fight you."

"You're threating us? If we kill you quick enough, you won't make it back to the Gravity Ring."

"The only good Apple's a dead Apple, I say."

I pressed the button three times and slowly backed away. "There's no need to..."

I found myself in amongst a number of tree stumps, though there were about twice as many large trees dotted around the area. I could see through the trees that I was now in the relatively flat part of the final half-bowl, the river perhaps two hundred metres to my right and the high rock columns about five hundred ahead of me.

There was a small sharp pain in my side as I turned, I looked down and found a significant tear in my clothes and a thin red line on my skin, though it wasn't bleeding.

Looks like I was a little better at dodging blows than that other guy.

In amongst the tall trees were some saplings and small trees, but none of them appeared to have any fruit on them. There were some small red fruit up in the tall trees, but all well out of reach.

Looks like all the easy stuff has been taken.

Then I noticed that the sound of splashing water that I was so used to hearing was not just in the distance to my right, but also in front of me. I rushed forward and found to my delight a small stream of clear water in a low trough.

I cupped my hands under a small waterfall and drank deeply of the cool water. It seemed to almost burn my parched throat as it rushed down, so I had to stop and take a few breaths until the drastic sensation faded, then drank deeply again, reveling in the refreshment it provided.

I sat back against the nearest tree and sighed. It felt good to just sit awhile after all of the frantic activity of the last few hours, or however long it was. The sun was quite a way above the horizon, but that didn't tell me much, since I had no idea how quickly it had been rising.

I looked back at the rock columns, there appeared to be wooden fences or fortifications of some kind around the tops of the columns with pairs of ropes strung from one summit to the next, as well as significant ground-level barricades in between the columns. There was also what appeared to be a line of dark bushes across the width of the ground in front of the columns.

Not exactly a welcoming sight. Rock Eaters? What sort of name is that?

I glanced back up the slope in the direction I had come, or rather towards the place I had been when I activated the beacon, and all thoughts of rest evaporated.

A band of five to ten men was already down the steepest part of the slope and was rapidly heading towards me, now two or three hundred metres from my position.

If the people who want me dead are afraid I'll join the Rock Eaters, then maybe I should be joining the Rock Eaters.

I stood and jumped across the trough, renewing the sharp pain in my side as I landed, then began making my way through the

179

trees, pressing against the injury with my left hand. The stiffness in my limbs was lessening and I tried to ignore the pain as much as I could, but I was still significantly slower than my pursuers.

Once we were both clear of the trees and into the half-kilometre of open ground, it was obvious that I would be caught before reaching the safety of the rocks, if they were safe at all.

What if the Rock Eaters are even worse than the Apples? What am I getting myself into now?

This new wave of discouragement slowed my progress further, and I rubbed my temples with my free hand, causing something metallic to bash into my nose and make my eyes water. I stopped in my tracks and blinked at the offending object.

The beacon! How could I forget it was there?

I quickly fumbled it into my palm and pressed the button three times.

I found myself at the foot of a rock column. Two metres behind me was the line of bushes, averaging a metre or so high and twice as wide, covered with large thorns. My pursuers were perhaps three hundred metres away, and still closing. The walls of the column were pockmarked, but basically vertical, and from down here the wooden fortifications at the summit appeared insurmountable.

This is safety?

I went down on all fours and scuttled over to the edge of the nearest bush, hoping that I would be suitably hidden from my pursuers, then began crawling in the direction of the river, which was three or four hundred metres away.

I heard the footfalls and chatter of my pursuers getting closer, and I crawled a little faster.

"Fan out, he can't have gone far."

I held still and pressed the beacon again three times. I found myself just where I was, only now I could hear my pursuers only a few metres away on the other side of the thornbushes.

Oh, crap. Move as quietly as you can, don't give your position away...

"Hey, you down there," called a voice from the top of the column. "What do you think you're doing?"

Double crap.

Chapter 9—The Rock Eaters

"He's a murderer," called a voice from the other side of the hedge. "Killed two of our men then thought he could escape to you using a beacon." Two of the others were probing for gaps in the bushes with their spears.

"Is that so?" called the voice at the top of the column. "Two men, all on his own?"

"Yes, he's a tricky one. Pretended to be all friendly and harmless, then when their guard was down gutted them with their own spears, left their blood all over the rocks."

"Very impressive."

"Look at his face, he's an Apple, taught to lie and kill and steal. Let us take him away and see that he faces justice."

"It would appear that he's not too keen on that idea. You down there, what do you have to say for yourself?"

I stayed silent, not wanting to give my position away.

"Ah, you think that if you speak up, your pursuers will find you and make you disappear?"

I nodded.

"And how many of them do you think will get out of here alive if they try that? I'll wager a loaf of bread on none. Bowmen ready!"

There were various creaking and clicking noises, and five men appeared at the top of the column, plus another ten or more at the top of the neighbouring ones, each with an arrow nocked in their bows.

"Now, if you gentlemen could kindly back away, go back home and let us deal with the newcomer, then nobody needs to get hurt."

"Have it your way," said the spokesman for my pursuers as they backed away, "but I wouldn't trust him if I were you, and definitely don't turn your back on him."

"Thank you for your cooperation and your concern, but you'll excuse us if we don't take your word for it, we like to judge for ourselves."

Silence reigned for a minute or so as the two separating sides watched each other and the tension in the air ebbed away, then the man at the top of the column called down to me.

"Alright, they're out of range and not coming back. What do you have to say for yourself?"

I slowly stood, peeked over the thorn bushes at the retreating forces for a few seconds, then turned to the man at the top of the column "I did face two men with spears, I was unarmed and it was on some rocks by the river. I also do carry the mark of an Apple, I'm sorry to say, I can't deny any of that. However I was tricked into joining the Apples and escaped from them at the first opportunity, nearly drowning in the attempt. I was trying to avoid a fight with those people and I activated the beacon before any blows were exchanged, so I have no memory of what happened in the fight itself, I only know that they injured me." I showed him the tear in my clothing, I didn't think he could see the wound from up there. "I don't want to cause any trouble, just to pass through to the lowest point, wherever that is. I know this doesn't sound very convincing..."

"You'd be surprised, I know the ring of truth when I hear it."

A rudimentary panel in the fortifications swung upwards and a knotted rope was unfurled down to me, ending half a metre or so off the floor. It was different from the ropes that the Apples used, it looked a lot rougher and more, natural?

"Up you come, then."

I walked up the column wall with the aid of the knotted rope, crawled through the gap and came face to face with a half-dozen men of all shapes and sizes. Some were wearing the same standard outfit as myself, others with additional or replacement crude pieces of clothing made from some sort of furry semi-rigid material. Some had the back half of their left cheek entirely filled in with blueberry markings, some had no markings at all, but each wore a proud yet warm smile on his face. They all had beards of various lengths, those with no markings having fuller facial hair than the others.

A short man with a somewhat rotund face and build extended his hand towards me, and spoke with the same voice I had heard before.

"Welcome to the Fortress."

"Thank you." I took the hand and stood, exchanged warm handshakes and welcoming greetings with the other five men, then took in my surroundings.

The fenced-in space at the top of the column was roughly five metres square, though it was more oval-shaped than anything, with a roughly octagonal wooden shelter with a thatched roof three metres across in the middle of it. A wispy line of smoke rose from a hole in the shelter's roof, and its main supporting stakes appeared to go deep into the rock itself, with extra little wooden wedges hammered in around them to secure them rigidly in place. There was a pile of rocks in one corner of the area, next to it a plastic box half full of water, and several shields and spears leaning against the outer fence.

"How did you do that? Drive stakes into the rock, I mean?"

"We have a special tool for that, which I can show you later."

Off to each side a set of three ropes, two thinner ones hung about half a metre apart and a metre above the third, were strung from the outer fence towards other rock columns and beyond. Beyond the column to the right was a large tree, to which the ropes were secured before continuing on, but its branches hid most of what was beyond that. To the left in the distance I caught sight of a much more massive rocky plateau with a fairly irregular shape.

"These ropes, they're very different from the ropes everyone else uses, not like the tent guide ropes. Did you make them yourself?"

He smiled and nodded. "It makes this whole fortress possible: the walls, the connecting lines, our weapons. We, or I should say our brothers across the river, make these ropes and twine from the plant that they cultivate on the far shore. In return we grow food for them and help to construct and repair their shelters. It is perhaps not even right to consider them different from us; we all inhabit and defend the fortress that spans the valley together, bound by the same code of honour, sharing knowledge, resources and cooperating on major projects."

"Grow food? You don't receive it from boxes?"

"Very rarely. Occasionally a box will arrive floating down the river, but they are usually empty, and we then use them for various purposes. One time when our harvests were weak and the leader of the Cherry tribe was a more reasonable man, he traded a box of food they had scavenged for some bows and arrows to defend his tribe with. Here we work to support ourselves, adapting and innovating as we go, it is a much more satisfying way to live."

He gestured to the other side of the fenced area and I walked over, looking down on a great field of what looked like golden wheat and beside that a series of furrows and ridges covered in low-lying green leaves of various shapes. The open area of ground itself was about three hundred metres wide, right up to the cliffs at the end of the valley, and perhaps a kilometre long, from the shores of the river to the massive plateau which merged with the cliffs. Beyond the river on the other side was another similar stretch of open ground, and beyond that another plateau. The open ground next to the river on that side was dominated by a thick 'forest' of tall thin stalky plants with spiky leaves, which looked to have grown to about twice the height of the people harvesting the adjacent plot.

The river bank on both sides was fortified with a sturdy-looking high wooden fence along both banks, though on the opposite bank it drifted a little way inland just before the river disappeared into the cliff face, where a fair amount of branches and other floating debris looked to have gathered.

"Why is there so much debris in the river there, and what is that detour in the fence?"

"There is a sloping metal grille across the whole opening that catches large objects while letting the water through, so we get a lot of building materials and most of our boxes that way, though they need to be cleaned. The detour is where the tunnel entrance is, I wouldn't go there if I were you."

"Tunnel? As in the lowest point and the way to the next stage?"

"Yes, but it's flooded all the way to the ceiling. The people we've tried sending in there either come back saying it's there's no way through or don't come back at all. We once tried tying a rope round an explorer's waist and sending him as far as he could go, but there was a great tug on the rope, it snapped and we never saw him again."

I gulped.

"But they wouldn't go to all this trouble just to kill us, would they? That makes no sense. I'd still like to see it for myself."

"We won't stop you from trying, but judging from all the grunting and groaning as you climbed up, I'd say you're in no fit state to make the attempt."

I glanced down at the floor. "That loud, was I?"

He sucked a little air through his teeth. "I'm afraid so. I'm sure some good food, drink, and rest will help with that, and in the meantime you can take a look around at what we've built here and see if it doesn't make you want to hang around for a while longer."

"As long as no-one tries to take my beacon."

"Why would we do that? We use them all the time."

I looked up and noticed that four of the six men were wearing beacons around their necks.

"You keep them? You're not worried about being thrown... wait, that doesn't happen, does it? What do you use them for?"

"As lights, of course. They may not seem like much in the day, but you'd be surprised how much of a difference they can make at night."

186

I was led along the rope bridge to the next column to the left, whose upper fortification layout was much the same. My guide turned to me as we moved past its shelter.

"Do you have a name?"

"The Apples called me Hookless, but I don't like that name. I hope to find my old name once I get out of here."

"Alright, then how about something more positive in the meantime, like, I don't know, Lifter? Raising moods, easing burdens, that sort of thing."

"Hmm," I nodded, feeling some of my inhibitions melt away. "That sounds a bit better, yeah, I suppose that'll do for now. What do they call you?"

"I'm Martin Grade."

I stopped where I was. "Wha- you remember your old name?"

"No, but once someone decides they're going to be here for the long term, the community comes together, they get a full name and we celebrate. Those are good days," he said with the kind of smile that made me want to see such an event for myself.

We moved on to the next column, then to the next, each of them a similar layout, though varying in size. After traversing five such columns, we arrived at the large plateau, which was around a hundred metres wide and three times as long, though with an irregular outline. The columns and their interconnecting bridges and barricades continued on into the distance, where the ground began sloping upwards towards the sides of the valley. The strip of lowland between the line of columns and the cliffs at the end of the valley was dotted with clumps of trees, partially hiding the wide stream that wound its way down the slope towards the base of the plateau.

The top of the plateau also had a fortification fence around it, and similar octagonal shelters of various sizes near its edges on top of the bare pockmarked rock, with its centre mostly empty. As we moved nearer the cliff side, there were also rows of simple low rectangular log frames a metre or so wide, most of them filled with earth in which various edible-looking plants were growing. Shallow staircases of what first appeared to be long hollowed logs, but most of which on closer inspection turned out to be half-pipes of fired clay, distributed water to various locations across the surface, presumably fed by the small waterfall at the left edge of where the plateau reached the cliffs. Towards the right end of the plateau there appeared to be a cave in the cliff wall, and next to the beds of earth around us was a strange roofless structure.

It was roughly circular and perhaps ten metres in diameter, comprised of a wide stone wall half a metre high that seemed to form the base of a three-metre fence of thick wooden stakes, all sloping inwards a little. Inhuman high-pitched noises that I couldn't quite place could be heard from the other side of the fence, and I felt mild prickles running up and down my spine. *And now we see what these people really are. What kind of twisted things are going on in there?*

"Um, what is that? A prison?"

Martin looked at me in utter bewilderment. "What? No." He then burst out laughing, shook his head, then beckoned with his left hand. "Come and see."

He walked over to a section of the fence next to where a short ladder lay on the ground, untied a short rope and swung up a panel of wooden stakes.

Inside the floor was much lower than the ground I was standing on, and gently sloped towards a crack in the rock on one side and away from what looked like a small cave on the other; the stone

188

wall was over two metres tall on the inside all the way round. There were three women in their thirties in the middle of the floor, surrounded by a flock of goats. One of the women was standing and hand-feeding several of the adults with various leaves and what looked to be the tops of carrots from a wooden container. The other two were seated on battered logs, caressing and feeding kids on their laps from what appeared to be canteens with some sort of teat stretched over their normal openings. Other young and adult goats were milling around them, nuzzling the women or chasing each other and generally appearing adorable.

I shook my head and smiled at how wrong I'd been.

"Now this structure took the most work out of anything we've built. There was a circular depression in the rock here and a crack on that side where the gap is, but we needed to hollow out the sides of the depression and build that wall to put the wooden stakes out of nibbling range. From experience, anything less than vertical walls will have them up and out of their enclosure, eating whatever greenery they find down to its roots."

"If they're that much trouble, why keep them?"

"Because their regular milk and occasional meat, skins and bones are worth it. And just look at them, you wouldn't believe how much our women love those little guys." The women looked up at us, smiled and waved. I couldn't help but smile and wave back.

"I can see that, and understand it," I said with a grin. *The Apples should have tried tempting me with this instead, but there's no way they could have built it.*

"We had to lift the goats up onto the plateau, the fact they couldn't get up here by themselves is a good sign for our defences. Some of them weren't too happy about being hoisted up, and the two most troublesome males ended up as the main course of the feast we held to celebrate completing the last fortification fence. That was another good day. Since then we've been reinforcing the barrier in various ways so enemy raids are even less effective.

"This has given us the space and stability to really invest time and resources in developing tricks and mechanisms to improve everyday things, such as our shelters, water supply, the food we eat and tools we use."

In between the planting beds was a long rectangular shelter with multiple doors along one side.

"This is our latrine," he gestured with pride.

I looked for signs of excavation under the structure. "You dug a hole that big in the rock?"

"No, after all the trouble with the goat pen we got smarter than that. You see all the earth in the beds around us?"

"Yes, that must have taken a huge amount of work to lift up here."

"Tell me about it. So that all that effort didn't go to just a single purpose, and to slightly reduce the amount of soil needed to fill the beds, the soil is first brought here, kept as dry as possible in one of those plastic boxes. A thin layer of earth is spread in the bottom of another box, which is then slid under the seats of the latrine, two over each box. When you do your business, you take a scoop of dry soil from here and add it to what you did, reducing the smell and at the same time fertilizing the soil. When the box gets full, we slide it out, empty it into one of the earth beds then start the process again. When the earth bed gets full, we plant it and construct a new one. No digging into the rock needed at all."

"Ingenious." I nodded.

"It took quite a bit of planning, implementing one of the many ideas outlined by our predecessors."

"Predecessors? How long has this community been going?"

"Our records go back five or more years, but those only began once we were stably enough established to have the time and resources to begin writing them, so who knows how long it has been since the first fugitive from a roving band clambered up the secluded rock chimney, discovered the cave and waterfall and set up his hidden camp. That cave is where we store our most precious possessions."

"Your stores of food?"

"Our stores of knowledge. Which plants can be eaten, and how to recognize, cultivate and prepare them; which structures are reliable and useful for various purposes and how to build and maintain them; which tools are best for various tasks and how to make and use them; the stories and songs of our people to gladden our hearts and lift our spirits. Our first archivists wrote in the margins and blank pages of the instruction manuals they brought with them, when space ran out they moved on to scratching them into the soft stone walls of the cave. It was only when we developed the means to manufacture our own paper and had people dedicated to maintaining and adding to our records that they surged in volume and quality, vastly improving our ability to build upon previous discoveries.

"Agriculture, fabric, fire containment, irrigation, bows and arrows, light reflectors, ladders, ropes and rope bridges, traversable cliff faces, all of these we have developed ourselves."

"Very impressive."

"Here we are, you can stay in this shelter and get some rest, I'll bring you some food."

The shelter was much the same as the ones on the column

191

towers, small log benches dotted around most of its circumference in between rough fabric bags of straw for sleeping on.

I lay down on a bag of straw and closed my eyes. It felt so good to rest my weary limbs. Perhaps I drifted off, because the next thing I knew Martin was back with a piece of flat bread and a steaming wooden bowl of some sort of stew. I couldn't tell what was in it, but it was very satisfying. A pair of peaches and a bunch of cherries followed, and I savoured the sweet flourish they provided to the meal.

"Thank you, Martin, that was very good."

"I'll pass on your compliments to the chef. Oh, there was one more thing, I'll go and get it." Martin disappeared through the shelter's doorway and came back with a small metal pot, half-filled with a familiar purple liquid...

I backed away. "What are you going to do with that?"

"Offer it to you."

"What for?"

"So you can blot out your Apple markings, if you want."

"Won't that make me one of you?"

"It doesn't have to. It'll just mean that you renounce your former allegiance, that you're nobody's property, and nobody has to know who you were allied with before. Just spread it on your cheek, obscuring whatever is there now. Over time it'll all fade to nothing."

I looked at the bowl, slowly reached out and dipped the fingers of my left hand in the sticky liquid, then smeared it all over the back of my left cheek, in my mind telling all the Apples to go and jump in the river. I looked up at Martin with half a smile.

"That felt good."

He smiled back. "I'll bet it did."

My smile faded a little. "I, I have a question, though."

"And what's that?"

"Now, I don't want to sound ungrateful, and I know you've all achieved a lot here, but isn't there more beyond the tunnel? Isn't there a much larger body of knowledge to build on out there, beyond this stage? Think of what we know they can do: they make all those boxes, tents, beacons, clothes and food; they construct truly astounding projects: the Gravity Ring, The White Space and this valley; they can even heal great injuries and wipe our memories. Who knows what else they can do, what we could be part of, if we just take that risk?"

"But here we have control of our destinies, here we are feared by the barbarians, we're making great progress and provide much needed stability to the valley. If we abandon all of this and risk the tunnel, what will happen to the fortress, to this haven, to this family? It will be occupied by a bloodthirsty tribe and used to terrorize everyone else here."

"I suppose so, but is this really meant to be our home, our final destination? They lured us out of the Gravity Ring with the promise of great adventures to be had and a real world to discover, and told us where to find the way out of here. There is clearly more to the real world than this valley, and out there is a world full of greater wonders than we can imagine.

"You have been here five, maybe ten years. How long have they been out there, a hundred, a thousand, ten thousand? If you can make all of this progress in the short time you have been here, just imagine how much progress they have made in theirs. You've made a lot of discoveries, I'll grant that, but do you really need to rediscover what they already know out there, and I assume are willing to share? Think of all the songs and stories they've written, the secrets they've discovered, places they've been, structures they've built and devices they've developed. That is something to explore and build on, out there, in the real world."

"Are you sure they would share? What if they are like the other tribes here? Everything we've toiled and sweated for, all we've achieved and worked to build and defend, it would be for nothing, sacrificed for a foolish hope. We would be nothing to them—a plaything, easy prey. I will take my chances here with the freedom we have built."

"But if this is where our journey is not supposed to end, then yes, you'll lose all you've built here, but with all the tenacity, industry and creativity you clearly possess, you'll be able to replace it all and more out there, won't you?"

"That's easy for you to say, you've invested nothing here. You haven't seen your plans come to fruition and felt the surge of pride when the last part is secured in place, your creation is put to use and the first beneficiary smiles in gratitude. Build with us, taste that joy and then tell me you want to leave it all behind."

I stared into space for a while as I considered the idea. *Risk the tunnel, or help these people? Flee the valley, or stay and build?*

I looked up at him.

"Alright. You seem to be good people, I hope you'll think the same of me. I had an idea that might help me live up to that name you gave me…"

To be continued...

About the Author

Ben Zwycky is an English ex-pat now living in the Czech

Republic. Before, during and after obtaining a masters in chemical engineering, he worked as a hospital porter, cleaner and server in a community centre, research assistant, EFL teacher and currently works as a freelance proof-reader and translator together with his Czech wife, who literally fell into his arms in the year 2000 and with whom he now has five children. His first novel, *Nobility Among Us*, is inspired in part by the country he now lives in, its many perfectly preserved medieval castles and chateaux standing side by side with modern constructions and technology. He is a regular contributor to superversiveSF.com and his poetry, occasional musings and other work can be found at benzwycky.com

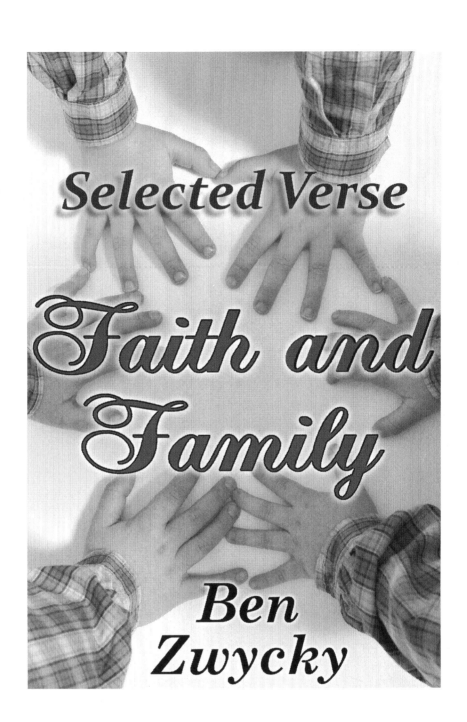

Selected Verse

Faith and Family

Ben
Zwycky

Reviews

A classic of the roman a clef, alternate-history, urban-fantasy 1940s Russia genre.

Peter S. Bradley

Wolfhound Century by Peter Higgins

Vissarion Lom is a police officer working for the state in this strange version of an alternate 1940s-era Russia. Lom lives in Lezarye, which around thirty to forty years earlier experienced some kind of take-over by the Vlast - a Russian word meaning "authority." The Vlast is presently governed by the Novozhd, an avuncular man, with a bushy mustache. The Vlast are at war with the Archipelago, which seems like a titanic struggle, involving massed attacks with planes and tanks. The Vlast maintain domestic control through informers, meticulous records of its citizens, and the willingness to liquidate troublesome members of society.

Clearly part of the fun is decoding the roman a clef of the story. Lezarye is Russia; the Novozhd is Stalin; the Vlast is the Communist Party. The capital of the Vlast is Mirgorod and seems to be St. Petersburg based on the story about how the "Founder" - Peter the Great, perhaps - founded it on the muddy marshes of the Mir. Likewise, the character Joseph Kantor may very well be a Lenin who didn't realize his destiny, although, if so, he shouldn't be a contemporary of the Novozhd, so, perhaps, he's Trotsky.

That's the familiar part, albeit any fantasy story based on Slavic roots is going to be alien, but then the world turns 90 degrees into fantasy. It seems that angels have been falling on Lezarye for the last 300 years. These angels seem to be gigantic beings who arrive dead. The angels don't seem to fall outside of Lezarye. Besides being awesome signs of something outside this earth, the flesh of the angels seem to have remarkable effects, the skin can be used to craft mudjhiks - from the Russian for "peasant" - golem death machines. There also seems to be a natural magic whereby some people can control the elements and the elements - wind and rain - have a personality. There are literal giants, suggesting - maybe - that the Nephilim didn't die out in this alternate history.

In addition, there is a strange kind of alternative-history, science fiction substory, as Vishnik, and some others, start to notice that the alternate history of a world without angels seems to be breaking through into their world.

Lom is reassigned from a dreary backwater far to the east of Lezarye, past the impenetrable forests, to Mirgorod in order to find a terrorist. The terrorist is Joseph Kantor, whose father led a rebellion and was executed. Kantor was sent to the gulag, escaped and made his way to Mirgorod. In Mirgorod, Kantor set up a terror cell and is apparently working for a living angel, trapped on earth, in the impenetrable forest, and the angel wants to escape. The angel sets Kantor the task of destroying the Pollandore, a seed of a possible future where there were no angels, crafted by the old gods before they fled in the face of the angels.

So, Lom is looking for Kantor and Kantor is looking for the Pollandore. Lom's pursuit of Kantor is assisted by the "deus ex author" of coincidence as Lom reunites with his old friend Vishnik. Vishnik knows Maroussia Shoumian, who knows Kantor, because he is - or is supposed to be - her father.

As Lom closes in on Kantor, all hell breaks loose in the Vlast. There are plots within plots as the angel's conspirators pull the trigger on their own power play. Lom and Maroussia go on the lam with the plan of activating the Pollandore. They get the help of a giant. There is giant versus golem action. Lom begins to remember that he shouldn't be as loyal to the Vlast as he has been...

..and then the story ends. This seems to be the first part of a multi-part story.

Fore-warned is fore-armed. If you are looking for a self-contained story, this is not it. I was surprised by the fact that this is only the first part of complete story. I think the book should have been clearly advertised as part one of a larger book.

In addition, it seems obvious from this review that the back-story is complicated, because there is so much going on with the alternate history tropes and the fantasy tropes. In contrast to the complex, crowded backstory, the main story of Lom looking for Kantor is comparatively simple, until the political coup happens, and then the unanswered question is, "what's going on?"

Obviously the answers will come in the next installment or installments.

For all the complexity, I liked the story. I liked the use of Russia as the departure point for this alt-hist/fantasy. I liked the use of Russian words and terms, which caused me to break out the dictionary. I found the author's writing to be clear, direct and engaging, and his use of short chapters keeps the story moving along. I became involved in Lom's story and I want to know where it goes after the end of this book. I want to know about the angels and the giants and the Pollandore and the rest of the complicated back-story.

So, since it kept my attention and made me want to follow the characters, I think that the book is worth my investment of time, and I'm giving it four stars.

The Science Fiction of History: Communism - Field Testing Science Fiction Plot Ideas since 1917

Peter Sean Bradley

The Plot to Kill God: Findings from the Soviet Experiment in Secularization by Paul Froese

Sometimes it seems that Communism was put on Earth solely for the purpose of trying out the crazy ideas of science fiction writers. Thus, imagine a society where people are born, live and die in a prison camp and you find North Korea. Imagine a culture that eliminates property and cash and you find the early Soviet Union under Lenin. Imagine "there's no heaven, above us only sky" and you have the 70 year history of the Soviet Union.

The Plot to Kill God by Paul Froese looks at the Soviet attempt to realize John Lennon's dream of a world without religion. Froese is a professor of Sociology at Baylor Universtity, so he obviously approaches what he calls the Soviet "Secularization Experiment" through the concepts, language, resources and models of Sociology.

He briefly reviews the relevant historical data - extreme repression of religion, repeated persecutions of religions, efforts by religious denominations to accommodate or resist atheistic Communism, all aimed at producing a secular, atheistic society where God was entirely forgotten - and asks whether the Secularization Experiment was successful, and, if not, why not?

Froese covers much of the same territory as that covered by Paul Gabel's "And God Created Lenin: Marxism vs Religion in Russia, 1917-1929." In fact, Froese uses Gabel as a source. Both books should be read by anyone interested in this subject. Between the two, Gabel does a better job of covering the historical detail, but Froese is much better at using the science of Sociology to model the reasons the Soviet experiment had the outcome it had.

In looking at the motivations behind the "Secularization Experiment," Froese destroys the conventional trope that Communist oppression of religion grew out of the political convictions and desire for power of Communists, rather than their atheist commitment. In a few deft strokes, Froese uses the fact that Communism sought to suppress all religions, including minority and powerless religions, to demonstrate that the Communist agenda was about God, not power. Froese observes:

> "Lenin equated religious traditions with social oppression because he believed that religious concepts tricked workers into accepting their fate. Lenin clearly asserted his disgust for religion: "Every religious idea, every idea of God, even flirting with the idea of God, is unutterable vileness... vileness of the most dangerous kind, 'contagion' of the most abominable kind. Millions of sins, filthy deeds, acts of violence and physical contagions... are far less dangerous than the subtle, spiritual idea of a God decked out in the smartest

"ideological" costumes... Every defense or justification of the idea of God, even the most refined, the best intentioned, is a justification of reaction." While Marx provided the philosophical and ethical justification for the demise of religion, Lenin additionally argued that enlightened individuals were morally obliged to destroy religion."

(The Plot to Kill God, p. 44.)

Froese explains the connection of Marxist ideology to the atheist project:

"From the start, Lenin demanded that Communist propaganda stress "militancy and irreconcilability towards all forms of idealism and religion. And that means that materialism organically reaches that consequence and perfection which in the language of philosophy is called—'militant atheism.'"

(The Plot to Kill God, p. 45.)

Froese deploys the concepts of "exclusivity" and "commitment" to explain Communism's militant atheism:

"Recent studies of religious groups find that "among religious organizations, there is a reciprocal relationship between the degree of lay commitment and the degree of exclusivity." Exclusivity refers to how prohibitive a religious group is in allowing commitment to other gods or religious doctrines. Religious groups often explicitly denounce other religious perspectives along with philosophical and political systems of belief that they feel contradict their theologies. Generally, religious organizations understand that exclusive theologies are more powerful than nonexclusive ones.

In contrast, openness to new ideas and tolerance of alternative views can lead to lower levels of commitment to a single ideology. All things being equal, the exclusivity of a doctrine is a primary determinant of its followers' devotion. As a humorist recently pointed out, suicide bombers don't tend to leave messages that state, "We are Unitarian Jihad. There is only one God, unless there is more than one God. The vote of our God subcommittee is 10-8 in favor of God, with two abstentions."

(The Plot to Kill God, p. 67.)

Communism was obviously an extremely exclusivist form of atheism.

Froese divides the analysis of the Secularization Experiment into "supply" and "demand." The Soviets were extremely successful in cutting off "religious supply" by destroying church hierarchies and confiscating property. The Soviets were less successful on the "demand" side. Their main effort in that regard was to mimic religious rituals. As Froese points out, devices like "Red Baptisms" and "Red Weddings" - and the constant atheist education - may simply have served to keep issues of God and religion alive in the minds of the Russian population.

Froese also points out that different regions and religions of Russia employed different strategies in their dealings with Communism. The Orthodox Church essentially sought to serve the Communist regime. Catholic Lithuania, in contrast, was able to resist Communism to a certain extent because of the loyalty of the Lithuanian population and the church's foreign support. Islamic Central Asia, on the other hand, embraced Communism as a way of modernizing its population. Although Communism abolished Islamic courts and rites, Islam was able to actually penetrate into the Communist party such that Communists self-identified as Muslims and vice-versa.

The Secularization Experiment was extensive. The League of Militant Atheists, followed by the Knowledge Society, took great efforts to educate and indoctrinate the Russian masses in atheism and the putative falsity of God and religion. As Froese explains, the Communists based their programs on assumptions that didn't stand the test of reality. For example, they believed that science would vanquish religion simply by showing that God was not in space. While we may think that the story of Yuri Gagarin saying that he could not see God in space, the Communists actually thought this was the nail in the coffin of religion. As Froese points out, this trades on a fundamental misunderstanding that God is an empirical fact in the world, something which believers did not believe.

One of the most fascinating and eye-opening parts of the book involves the return of religion after the fall of the Soviet Union. As Froese points out, prior to the fall of Communism, approximately 20% of the Soviet population claimed to be atheist. Within a few years of the Communist collapse, this percentage had dropped to less than 4%, and by ten years to 1 to 2%. As Froese explains:

> These data highlight the failure of scientific atheism to establish committed followers. In other words, atheist education and propaganda had no lasting effect on the belief system of most Communist citizens.

(The Plot to Kill God, p. 126; See also p. 177.)

Why had the Secularization Experiment failed so spectacularly? Froese examines the usual sociological theories behind the idea that secularization is an inevitable outgrowth of science or progress or education, or that religion can simply be replaced by similar-looking rituals, and finds those assumptions empirically wanting. It seems that in any population there is an inherent demand for religion - for reasons we do not now know - and that while intense pressure may disrupt the expression of religious demand, or distort religious demand, that demand, apparently, remains.

What the Secularization Experiment did was to destroy "religious capital." Religious capital is the knowledge and practice of particular religious traditions. Muslims in Central Asia, for example, had to relearn Islam after Communism in the same way that the Orthodox had to relearn Christianity. One of the ironic features that Froese points out is that after 70 years of Communism, the net result was the re-establishment of "weak monopolies" of the original denominations in their respective parts of the old Soviet Union.

At the end of the book, Froese gives useful advice to would-be dictators - don't fight God, co-opt Him. Use the Western European model of weak religious monopolies and the established church may turn out to be a bulwark of your regime. As Froese points out:

> After the revolutions of 1989, theorists naturally set about trying to make sense of these seemingly unique and largely unpredicted events. The result was a myriad of narrative explanations to uncover the causal mechanisms that produced these specific revolutions. Certainly, many scholars stress Soviet Communism's inability to compete with the economic success of Western capitalism. But most agree that the Communist regimes ultimately fell because they lost their legitimacy. in other words, much of the public simply had no faith in the social system, and their distrust pushed low-level political and economic instability to the point of collapse.

(The Plot to Kill God, p. 176.)

So, ironically, it was the Communist "lack of faith" that ultimately

208

destroyed Communism.

Of course, this "solution" is problematic. It was the exclusive faith of atheistic Communism - which could brook no rival - that led to its success. One suspects that the logic of such an exclusive atheist ideology would have prevented it from tolerating a rival like God, particularly since it was the existence of an opposition center of power in the Polish Catholic Church that ultimately brought it down.

This is an excellent and highly readable book. If I have one nit to pick, it would be that I wish that Froese had gone back to original sources for his quotes from Lenin, Marx and other Bolshevik leaders. It seems that he relied on a lot of secondary sources, albeit well-respected sources, such as Robert Conquest. This will not be a concern for most readers, but I have a mania for reading the original source and now I have to go to Conquest to check his footnotes to find the original source.

That said, this book is a fruitful source of insight. For example, Froese makes the almost throwaway comment that attempts to build religious utopias are almost always more human than attempts to build secular utopias, because religious utopias don't expect to find perfection in this world, but, by definition, a secular utopia that doesn't produce results sometime in this world is a failure. (p. 140.)

A great deal of 20th century history is captured by that observation.

Classic Science Fiction - Phil Marlowe among the Stars

By Peter S. Bradley

The Winds of Gath: The Dumarest Saga Book 1 by E.C. Tubbs

It is a hard, harsh and corrupt universe that Earl Dumarest inhabits. He wakes up three days early from "cold sleep" with good news and bad news. The good news is that he survived - yet again - the one in eight mortality rate associated with "riding low" along with the farm animals and other people too poor to travel in space awake. The bad news is that his space ship has been re-routed to the armpit of the galaxy - a world named Gath, which is a poor place with no jobs, little food, no way off and only one reason people travel to Gath, to experience the haunting, psychosis-inducing music generated by an oddly-formed mountain range when the "winds of Gath" start blowing.

Dumarest is ejected to the planet and runs into his friend, Megan, so maybe it's not such a big universe after all. Dumarest fails at fishing, because the fishes are apparently more interested in eating "Travelers" like Dumarest, fishing for them on flimsy rafts, than being served up for dinner. Starving and desperate, Dumarest fights a battle to the death with a trained fighter of the Prince of Emmend for the entertainment of the decadent wealthy. Dumarest

211

wins, which is fortunate, or we wouldn't have the next 34 books in the Dumarest of Terra series, and then he's sucked into the high politics of the tiny world of Gath.

Dumarest is then introduced to the Matriarch of Kundar, who is visiting Gath with her ward, the Lady Seena, who may be her heir apparent. The Matriarch is served by a Cyclan - a human being trained and surgically altered to be emotionless and a cog of a great scheming organization. The Prince of Emmened may hold a grudge against Dumarest, but he definitely has his eyes on the Lady Seena. The Factor of Gath is not above turning men into beasts for a few bucks. In the middle of this, the Brotherhood arrives on Gath, bringing their commitment to charity and humanity as a rare, rare bit of kindness in this brutal universe.

In *The Winds of Gath*, E.C. Tubb introduces the main clichés that will dominate and drive Dumarest through the next 34 books. Dumarest wants to return to his lost homeworld, a world that everyone denies exists, called "Earth." The Cyclan seem to be hostile to Dumarest for no immediately apparent reason. The Brotherhood is there to provide support. The wealthy one percent treats the poor as subhuman objects to exploit for labor and entertainment.

This is the pulpiest of pulp science fiction, and, yet, it will grow on you as you follow Dumarest over the series.

Tubb barely begins to sketch the sociology of his universe. Tubb's sociology remains very simplistic throughout the series. There are always the very wealthy, corrupt, rich movers and shakers, and there is a grasping, greedy mercantile class, and below it all are the poor, including the transient Travelers, who move from star to star as the whim takes them. No matter the world, no matter what incidental sociological overlay Tubb tosses in - be it a matriarchy or some other social system - power and oppression is the reality that Dumarest experiences.

Finally, there is Earl Dumarest. It occurred to me on re-reading that Dumarest seems to be most akin to Raymond Chandler's detective, Philip Marlowe. Like Marlowe, Dumarest lives in a corrupt world where it would be most comfortable to become a craven toady to some corrupt, bestial, powerful imbecile. But, again, like Marlowe, Dumarest won't compromise, as he threads his way through a barely seen game of shadows played by some very obscure rules.

What was interesting about this first Dumarest novel was how inexperienced Dumarest was. I remember him from the later books when he'd seen it all and done it all as "uber-competent." In this book, he doesn't seem to have the rules down. Dumarest's chief power - apart from his near-mutant reflexes and ability to absorb pain - is his luck. In this book in particular, it seemed that he was really, really lucky in ways that had nothing to do with his being prepared to exploit the breaks that came his way.

All in all, it was a quick read and fairly satisfying. For someone not acquainted with the series, it probably will seem like a "bleh" experience, but it passes the time, and if you're looking for an existential hero in a book with fairly predictable pacing, this is a good book to kill some time with.

An entertaining mystery, but not a fantastic fantasy

By Peter S. Bradley

The Mystery of Grace by Charles de Lint

Unlike a lot of urban fantasies, which are clichés built on tropes, Charles De Lint's *The Mystery of Grace* kept me entertained all the way to the end, which is why I gave it 4 stars on Amazon.

The strength of *The Mystery of Grace* is that there is a bona fide mystery in the story that I wanted explained, namely Why does Grace's after-life world only extend several blocks from the Alverson Arms apartment where she lived before her death. This mystery does get explained and resolved in a satisfactory way.

A further strength is de Lint's use of the American Southwest as the setting for the development of the characters and their worldview, which includes abuelos and saints and Our Lady of Altagracia.

The opening was particularly effective, where de Lint set up the mystery of the disappearing tattooed girl. The prose grabbed me and the scene was a hook that set up the book. Charles de Lint is a good writer from a technical standpoint, and his prose is satisfying and pleasant to follow.

On the other hand, the story was disappointing in the mundaneness of life after death. When Grace returns for her biannual jaunt into the world of the living, it's not very haunting. Grace is the same person she was before she died. I take it that the banality of the supernatural world followed from de Lint's decision to write the story from Grace's perspective. It is undoubtedly very hard (or impossible) to write a story where the first person narrator is mysterious and spooky to herself.

Likewise, de Lint's nods to multi-culturalism, where everyone is right in their understanding of the mystery of life, so long as they believe in their own faith, seemed to strengthen the shallowness of Grace's after-life world - it was as if we are finally given the answer to the great mystery of life after death and find out that the answer is the slogan "Do your own thing." For example, there is a scene where the residents of the Alverson Arms world confront the McGuffin of the story with their own objects of faith, which for one person - an atheist, I assume - was a copy of Darwin's Descent of Man. This seemed to me to point out the problem of a deracinated supernatural world. To put it bluntly, when I read this scene, my thinking went something like: "For heaven's sake! This guy is dead, he has empirical, experiential proof of a reality beyond the material world, and he is still an atheist?????"

De Lint was much better, in my opinion, when he was writing from the perspective of Grace and Conchita's folk Catholicism, because at least then, there seemed to be some rules for the supernatural world that might have provided a depth and texture to that world. At least when Grace was asking for Our Lady's protection, I had a sense of a mysterious supernatural world that beckoned to my imagination.

Nonetheless, my philosophical/theological quibbles aside, it was a fun book and I felt that I got my money's worth of entertainment

216

value from it.

Made in the USA
Lexington, KY
08 May 2015